Son of the Right Hand

by John Baltisberger

An Aggadah Try It Publication

Madness Heart Press
2006 Idlewilde Run Dr.
Austin, Texas 78744

First Edition
www.madnessheart.press

Dedicated to Lisa Lee and Mitchell who have stood by me, cheered me on, and championed my work throughout it all. You two are amazing, and I wouldn't be half the writer without Lisa's dedicated and amazing editing skills.

Chapter 1

When I was a kid, I idolized the noir detectives of the 1940s, the private eyes that would sit in smoke filled offices and make small talk with leggy blonds in heavy East Coast accents. It had been an awakening of sorts for me. I wanted to be a cool, sophisticated gumshoe, charismatic in a way that only men from the 1940s thought men should be charismatic. Instead, I had been stuck on a ranch in North Texas watching cows and horses swat at flies. Most of my friends' favorite game was playing toss the cow patty. Not quite the smoke filled mystique I craved.

I wish I had known how good I had it back then. The office was the best part of that fantasy, and when actually doing the kind of work that I, to this day, imagine those detectives doing, I kvetched every second. The car stank of stale coffee and long nights. Wrappers from fast food burgers littered my passenger seat, and I worried I would be gaining all the weight I had managed to lose during my hospital stay. It had taken me just a couple of months to turn my new car into a mess. But I didn't exactly have a lot of good options. APD had wrapped up their investigation of Basken's cult of occultists. They assumed that all the dead and all of the members had been accounted for. My guess is that it was because of whatever lies Basken was spinning from his cell. A normal criminal would probably hand over his underlings in a heartbeat to get a leaner sentence, to avoid hardship, but I think people like Basken—mages, necromancers, and cultists—they feel like it's more important for their work to continue. So long as the police didn't catch them all, there would still be necromancers out there endangering the community at large and, more specifically, me.

So, I had been following up, using a mix of divination and good old-fashioned internet sleuthing to track down the remnants of the Basken cult. Well, I didn't do the internet sleuthing, I left that to people who were more tech savvy than I was, which was mostly everyone.

My phone chimed silently, the screen lighting up the interior of the car in bright ugly light. Anyone looking in my car would have seen me then, a disheveled Jew with brown close-cropped hair, a beard that was beginning to look less scruffy and more managed, and sunken green eyes that would look more at home in a raccoon than a man. I was wearing my normal dark suit, though my tallit katan and my kippah were tucked in the glove compartment rather than on my person at the moment—they had been on the seat next to me, but I felt guilty about the food debris. I grabbed my phone and turned down the brightness as much as it would go and looked at the screen, fearing that Sara was about to lecture me on leaving my girlfriend alone so many nights in a row. Instead, I was greeted by a text from an unknown number.

Esuriit et Mortuus Est - Johann Velk

A book title and author, another text from Grin. Mr. Grin was a ghoul hitman who had discovered not only where I lived but where my family lived when I had crossed their king Baalrachius during the Basken fiasco. I hated the idea of ghouls using technology. I had only met two that wore more than rags. They all seemed so feral and bestial that it was almost laughable picturing the canid Mr. Grin leaning against a wall or sitting on a toilet texting away with his too long talon-tipped fingers. Almost. For weeks, the homicidal Grin had been sending me after items and books. Each one had turned out to be some sort of tome of magic or grimoire of demonic and dangerous entities. The things I had been able to get my hands on so far I had locked in a safe in my workshop space. They were treif, dangerous base things that were dangerous for the world at large ... and my soul in particular. I hadn't decided what to do about them yet. I couldn't hand them over to Grin; even in the right hands, these items were too corrupt, and in his claws, they could be devastating.

I set the phone down and looked back out towards the rows of houses. There had been a time when Round Rock, Texas had been a suburb, a small nothing with a couple of stores; but now it was an extension of Austin, a tendril of development and wealth reaching out to swallow more of the Earth like the hungry maw of some destructive swarm. But it was nice, white picket fence nice. The sort of nice where they didn't let people like me into their golf clubs. My musings on the nature of urban sprawl and development was interrupted by movement. Finally.

Two men were leaving the house on the corner. The house I had been watching every night for nearly a week. Alan Attback and Ansar Mullhani, every bit of magic and research I had thrown their way had returned with warning signs and dire omens of wrong doing. Each of them had been in close contact with Basken in the weeks leading up to the ritual I had interrupted. Unfortunately, a call to the police consisting of 'I cast stones carved with the alefbet and spied on some people using cybercrime' was not usually a good path to walk in getting what you wanted. So here I was. But now that they were leaving, I could break in, find something incriminating, and fabricate a reason for the cops to show up and drag the remainder of Basken's sycophants into custody. I watched the two men pile into the car and drive off. I was wary. It was possible that this was a commune, some sort of group home, and there could be more of them inside. The house was in the name of Attback, but from everything I had witnessed, Mullhani lived there too. I hadn't seen anyone else during my time staking out the home, but I also hadn't seen both men leave at the same time before.

If I was going to have a chance, this was it. I opened the door and stretched. I left my gun in its holster under the driver's seat. If something went wrong, being caught breaking in with a gun would look much more suspect, though I doubted the brass knuckles and butterfly knife I had in my coat would look great. But they would be easier to lose and replace if I had to. I scanned the street warily. While I was hunting down explicitly bad people, no witness would understand that, and all it would take was one overzealous neighbor calling the cops to make my night end in disaster.

Crossing the street quickly, I looked around one last time for any unwanted eyes before pulling open the house's back yard gate and slipping in. I was almost surprised when I discovered the gate swung with no lock. I would have assumed anyone hiding shady business would be more careful, or at least more secretive than that. But as usual, those that dabbled in the supernatural rarely considered the more mundane threats. I guess that was me, a mundane threat. I shut the gate behind me and started looking for ways to get inside the house.

Breaking and entering … I wondered idly what my mother would think of this. Would she feel differently if she knew why? Would she care? My mother was an amazing woman, strong enough to raise a couple of Jewish kids in bum-fuck Texas, strong enough to tame a cowboy and to weather his death. I paused in my survey as I thought about my mother and the kind of life my sisters and I had levied on her. Kim had walked a rough path, diving into drugs and rock n roll, and even when she occasionally got clean, it was pretty clear she just plain didn't like children. Sammy had announced fairly early in life that men were not for her and worn her rainbow pride ever since. Mom didn't care, not about that, but it did mean that, to her, I was the only chance at the grandchildren she so desperately wanted. But my life, one of hunting monsters and mad men in the shadows of civilized Jewish society, meant that I had very little opportunity to really settle down. It meant that I had to balance trying to build a life with Sara with the lying to her regularly about what it was I did day in and day out.

I didn't think Sara knew; how could she? Who would guess that their boyfriend was secretly out there fighting necromancers and ghouls and whatever else the world of shadows threw against him? But she knew something was up, she was smart like that, and ever since my hospitalization after the confrontation with Basken, I had felt the tension there, bubbling just under the surface.

I shook off my thoughts of family and the tension between me and Sara and focused on the task at hand. I crossed the overgrown yard, listening carefully for any sounds that might indicate a guard dog, other inhabitants, or any other form of security. On top of the mundane, I scanned the tall grass for more unconventional means of defense. Lucky for me, I had taken only three steps when I caught the dull glint of metal in the weeds. Bending over to inspect it, I was treated to a view of an honest to G-d bear trap. I stood up and looked over the rest of the path to the house. One false step and I could say goodbye to my leg; and lest I forget, these were practitioners of dark magic on top of everything else.

I lifted my hands, murmuring a prayer under my breath, willing the unseen and hidden out into the open. The prayer was a short one, but I repeated it, the words falling out of my mouth in a droning chant. Each time around, I emphasized different syllables of the Hebrew, keeping my mind actively on the process of praying, focusing my intention on the space before me, then I spread my arms, a glittering web of power manifesting in my mind's eye and stretching between my fingers. With a thought, I spread the web outward, allowing it to float down and coat the backyard. Within a few seconds, the web faded from my imagination, but where it had touched traps and cantrips, I felt the dull heaviness of aggression. I wondered what would happen to me if I had stepped in that trap? Would I have been left to bleed out? Would I have been taken to prison or shot where I lie? No use in guessing at the minds of mad men. I stepped up to the sliding glass backdoor and peered through to the interior of the home.

It looked like a frat house to me, discarded to-go boxes and cold pizza left on tables. The lack of booze would have tipped me off that maybe kids didn't live here, but they were definitely slobs. I shook my head and tried the door. Locked. I had once tried to learn lock picking; it hadn't worked out in my favor. I just didn't have the manual dexterity for it. So instead, I decided to handle this the old-fashioned way. I wrapped my gloved hand in my sleeve, trying to get some protection, and moved to the window next to the door. One swing cracked through the glass, and then it was easy enough to reach through, pop the lock, and push the window open. A moment later, I was standing in the spider's den.

✡

It smelled as bad as it looked, old, stale, and moldy food, but underneath that was an antiseptic hint that made me think that somewhere in this home they had been busy cleaning ... something. I moved through the house. I wasn't even sure what I was looking for, to be honest. It wasn't like they would have a big book of crime or a dead body lying around. I suppose my plan was to find something illegal, put it in the front window, and then call the cops, giving them a reason to search the place more fully. And hopefully, they might fight something that would connect the two men to the killings.

I was in the living room poking through papers when I heard what sounded like crying. The worst-case scenario, the men weren't living here alone. I assumed the crying voice belonged to someone hiding from me who was afraid. Maybe Attback and Mullhani didn't bring anything illegal here. Maybe whoever else was here was completely innocent and terrified of a home invader. I moved as quickly and quietly as I could towards the backdoor. I could get out, get back to my car, and hopefully get out of the neighborhood before anyone from law enforcement showed up. I was almost there when I realized there was another, more sinister possibility ... the crying could belong to some trapped spirit, held captive by the men for ghastly rituals. I turned back towards the interior of the house, juggling in my mind if I should risk exposing myself. But I don't do this work because I play things safe.

I crept down the hallway towards the sounds of weeping, more and more sure this was a person and not some trapped spirit. They must have heard me breaking the window and gone to hide. Still, something pulled at me to keep moving forward. In the middle of the hall, I found a door that was dead-bolted from the outside. The sounds of choked sobs leaked out from under that door. This was worse, this was worse than a spirit I could release or a cultist hiding from me. A hostage. This was someone who they were holding against their will. Why? Someone who broke ranks? Someone who they kidnapped? My stomach lurched at the thought of leaving them alone here. They could kill her, at least! It was more probable they had already done terrible things to whoever was in there. I hadn't seen them bring anyone else home, which meant the victim behind this door had already been alone with the two practitioners of debased magic for quite some time.

My hand hovered over the lock for a moment. A living person would have to be rescued; they would be noisy, need protection. They would need help, and I wouldn't be able to just call the cops, I would have to explain why I broke in. A person behind this door meant things were about to get very complicated. But there wasn't really any question on the right course of action. I pulled the lock back and swung the door in.

✡

The smell of ammonia and other anti-septic chemicals hit me like a hammer to the face. It was followed by a strong undercurrent of feces, making my eyes water. The sobbing had choked off, and now it sounded like someone was screaming, but it sounded muffled. As though they were screaming from around a gag. I reached out, searching for a light switch, unwilling to face the muffled shouts and chemical smell in the dark. Once I got the light on, I wished I hadn't.

The room was large, probably a bedroom originally, but the carpet had been torn up. Normally, I'm pretty decent about checking the corners of rooms, sweeping a setting for threats, it's one reason I've survived as long as I have, but the centerpiece of this room demanded my full attention immediately.

In the center of the room was a large statue of a multi-limbed woman, her nude form both inviting and terrifying. I felt like the cold dead eyes of the statue were watching me, that there was an intelligence beyond the stone the statue was made of. Two of its arms reached up. Two supported the almost comically large breasts the sculptor had given the caricature of the woman. The last two reached down and held chains, chains which ended in shackles holding a wide-eyed, terrified woman, the source of the sobs and screams.

Her brown hair was matted to her face and head, and she looked filthy. Her hands were stretched above her head as she hung from the shackled grip of the statue. Blood, both fresh and dried, coated her arms, dripping from her wrists, injured and re-injured every time she struggled. She wore what had probably at one point been a perfectly pretty sun dress but now was a ruin of blood, dirt, and ...

she was sitting in her own filth. It looked like her captors didn't care all that much about keeping things tidy. A bright bit of cloth had been jammed in her mouth and tied to keep her quiet.

I rushed to her side and started looking over the manacles that held her. She, for her part, pulled away from me in abject terror. I could only guess what horrors they had visited upon the poor woman.

"I'm not here to hurt you. I'm going to get you out of here." My hands fumbled at the shackles, looking for some release mechanism, before giving up and pulling the wadded fabric from her mouth. This was nightmarish. In the back of my head, imagery from my time during the 2006 Israel-Hezbollah War threatened to swell forward and swallow me whole, but I pushed it back; it wasn't useful now. It never was, but it was particularly unwelcome right now.

"Oh god, oh god, oh god, oh god, oh god, oh god, ohgodohgodohgodohgodohgodohgod" The woman's voice was cracked and hoarse, dry from screaming and pleading and crying. Her eyes were puffy from tears shed and the fumes that where everywhere.

I nodded in agreement.

"I know, I know. Look at me." I waited until her eyes, which rolled madly in her head, focused on my face for a moment before continuing. "I'm going to get you out of here. They won't touch you again. Do you know where a key is? Do you know how I can get you out of here?"

"Back there, they always went back there." She lifted a finger and pointed towards the right side of the room.

I pulled my eyes from her wounds and turned to look. Other than the strange altar the woman was strapped to, the room was filled with a maze of shelves, and on each shelf sat jars of preserved organs. It looked like the inside of an oddities market, though I suspected these organs were probably sourced locally. I nodded and moved around the shelves in the direction she had pointed. There on a small shelf was a collection of items. A wallet with the woman's ID in it, Kristine Wallace, and Kristine's car keys, a backpack, and ... panties that were ripped. I swallowed the pain and disgust that threatened to overtake me. Losing my cool wouldn't help Kristine at all, and so I shoved everything I saw into the backpack until I found a small metal key. It looked like it might be what I was looking for. I tossed the backpack over my shoulder and turned back and wove through the shelves of grisly trophies. As I rounded the shelf, I was brought up short and dropped the backpack where I stood.

The statue had moved, not something subtle either, it had turned to face me. The top two arms snaked slowly through the air, the bottom two had risen, yanking Kristine Wallace off the ground and dangling her. One of its middle hands covered her mouth in a vice grip of stone, the other traveled over Kristine's body like a lover's caress. I could barely hear Kristine's screams from under the stone hand, but the way she writhed and tried to escape the hand spoke volumes of the wrongness I was watching.

I reached slowly into my coat, pushing the brass knuckles onto my fingers, aware that the eyes of the statue were on me. They glittered like gemstones, with mischief, as though the torture of this poor woman was a game, some sort of sick foreplay before the real fun began. I took one step closer, and the statue—or whatever it was—smiled. Stone lips that somehow gave the impression of a soft plumpness gasped in pleasure at my approach. It was a profane thing; it mixed seduction with cruelty in a way that I wasn't ready for. I took another step forward, trying to figure out what in HaShem's name this thing was. It didn't seem to be undead, though I supposed there could be a corpse tucked away inside the statue, and it certainly wasn't a golem as I understood them.

"You want to know what I am." It wasn't a question.

"No, I want you to let the girl go," I corrected.

The thing was reading my thoughts. I quickly began running a psalm through my head to drown out anything else it could glean.

"The girl, this girl? Oh, why would I do that? She is a most precious gift, an offering on the altar of blood and lust and filth that can be savored for ages."

I took a step forward, and the statue responded by viciously digging its claws into the woman's abdomen. I froze. I couldn't stay here long; I had to save the woman and get out of here before the cultists came back. And calling the cops was out, this creature would kill anyone who came in here—and all of that was assuming she didn't kill me before I had a chance to escape. My eyes looked over the room, looking for a weapon or a tool or anything that could help.

"You are worried about time. Do not worry. It will take more than some crazy cult to take you down, Ze'ev." The smile on the statue's face was cruel and wide.

When it said my name, I winced. I wasn't surprised it knew who I was, I had taken down their leader and been a target for them. But it was never pleasant when a monster said your name.

"Just trying to make a plan," I admitted.

"Ah, well then, plan around this." With a deft movement, the statue lifted its hand away from

Kristine's body and gripped her head. Before I could react, the statue brought its hands together, pulping Kristine's skull in the span a heartbeat. Blood and brain matter splattered across the room, forcing me to shut my eyes against the sudden gory rain. I felt teeth tap against me as they flew out from the force and speed of the violence. It took me a moment to realize that I was screaming. The mess of hair and bone tissue oozed between the statue's fingers, down into the gurgling throat, and the tongue, unconstrained by upper or lower jaws, lashed about in its death throes. The statue opened its hands, releasing the chains and allowing the corpse to fall back into its fecal mound of waste and blood.

I launched myself forward, bringing the sigil-engraved brass knuckles around in a wild swing. It was a blind rage. I didn't know what I hoped to accomplish, if anything. I shouted a letter, too enraged by the violence—and, if I was honest, by my powerlessness to stop it—to care about the ramifications of invoking the true power of the creative alefbet. With the true pronunciation of Gimmel, I invoked Gabriel and gabor, strength. For a moment, I was the sledge hammer, the wrecking ball of HaShem. I struck the statue with the force of creation's fury. The stone under my fist was pulverized, dust and debris flying outward, unintentionally mirroring the violence done to poor Kristine, z'l.

The power of the alefbet is fleeting. It can be sustained through intense concentration and intention, but invoked the way I did it, with passion and rage, it was instantaneous, a flash of all the strength one could ever hope for, and then it was gone. Like adrenaline wearing off, I collapsed next to Kristine's corpse. The statue lay in dozens of pieces across the room, but still the mouth moved in soft words of mockery.

"Oh, poor little wolf. You think you are tying off loose ends, but this is only the beginning, we are only just getting started. As one thing ends, another rises to take its place. You are but a pawn in a war that stretches back through pre-history."

My body ached. Every muscle felt torn and used up from my brief infusion of creative and destructive energy. But I had to move, I had to rise and get out of there. I pushed myself off the floor, and my hands squelched in the remains and leavings of poor Kristine. I knew her death would haunt me. I would always wonder if there was something more I could have done, anything I could have said that would have had a different result. I hated that people had died because of me.

And that this wasn't the first.

During my tangle with Basken, I knew of at least three people Basken had murdered simply to use their corpses to get back at me—a zombie, a ghost, and a frame job. I was tired of all the death. I looked away from Kristine's corpse; it wasn't how she would have wanted to be known or remembered. I had to get out of there, I could make sure her family had closure, and I could make sure that these sick sons of bitches paid the price for their crimes. With new motivation, I pushed myself off the ground and made my way towards the back door. My body fought me every step of the way, my muscles and bones demanding rest, punishing me for my haphazard use of holy language. It wasn't as bad as other incantations or uses of the alefbet, but it wasn't fun.

I fought through the exhaustion, stumbling through the backyard with only my memory to remind me where the traps were. I was lucky to make it out in one piece. But I still had to make my way as inconspicuously as possible back to my car and call the police. I think I did fairly well; no one came running out to demand to know who I was, no one stopped me. Once I was back in my car, I popped the trunk and threw in my now filthy coat. I had to get home and clean off. As I drove home, I used a burner phone—a habit I picked up after Basken had caused my last cell phone to be haunted by an angry dybbuk—and called 911 to get the police.

I described hearing screams and fighting and said I could have sworn I saw someone stumble out of the house with blood on their hands. Hopefully, it would be enough to spur an investigation, and hopefully, no one had gotten my license plate as I left. I drove as carefully, as safely as I could while trying not to fall asleep at the wheel. I needed a shower—I needed a *hot* shower—and to sleep until next week.

Chapter 2

I didn't get to sleep for a week, I barely slept that night, instead watching the news as the hammer came down. I had to imagine it had been a strange moment for the news and the police. Anonymous call turns out to be a horrifying bloodbath, ritual killings, dead bodies, the whole works all in a sleepy little white picket fence neighborhood. Of course, people were still on edge from the big bust of the cult earlier in the year, so as soon as some cop leaked news of the ritual killing to the media, they were all over the house like flies on shit.

It sounded like the police had gotten to the house and started the media vortex of insanity before Attback or Mullhani had come home. Their faces were plastered across the screen there for everyone to see, to know they were pieces of murderous shit. They would be hunted down and maybe made an example of. I had grabbed a takeout box of lo mein from the fridge to nosh on as I watched, but it had set on my table untouched since the news began. I realized my hands were balled into angry fists. I was wishing harm on these men, not so that they wouldn't hurt anyone else but for the hurt they had already caused, for what they did to Kristine.

I forced my hands flat on my legs. When was the last good night's sleep I'd had? How many deaths did I have on my hands now? Too many. Too many and now there was more, almost more than I could bear. I wasn't hungry anymore; the lo mein wasn't doing the trick. I pushed it back into the fridge and grabbed my phone—my actual phone, the one I had neglected for a week or so while tracking down the remainder of the cult before walking out of my apartment. I had started sleeping here again almost exclusively after Grin had visited me. I knew he was aware of Sara and my mother, but that didn't mean I had to put them in more danger by spending my nights in their houses. Besides, there was something nice about having my own space, even if my own space had become a hotbed of break-ins and death threats. I looked up at the night sky. I lived too close to downtown Austin to be able to really see the stars any more, a pity, since when I was younger, the night would have been alive with the twinkling of celestial bodies.

I wasn't sure where I was walking, I just let me legs carry me forward, no goal in mind, just trying to walk enough that I could banish my anger and the underlying grief for a woman who I didn't know but couldn't save. I wanted to walk until I collapsed. Maybe if my body could no longer sustain the momentum, it would let me sleep without seeing a woman's head shatter in the vice grip of a living statue. In the silence, I heard the drip of her cranial fluids leaving between the squeezing gore drenched fingers that had killer her. I didn't want that, but I knew these would be my new companions, a brand new destination for the nightmares that were as much a part of me as breathing or praying.

"Hineyni. Ani haba," I muttered. *I am here, I came.* I don't know who I was talking to, but I surrendered to the feeling of despair. I knew when I looked at my phone, I would have new missed messages—from Sara, from Nathan at the Beit Din, probably my mom or sisters ... Eventually, I had to get back to the world. But I was terrified the supernal terror that existed in my secret life would infect the life I lived in the sunlight. My fingers played over the screen and corners of the phone in my pocket. Would it make a difference? If I tried to keep them separate, eventually something like Mr. Grin or Basken would force the issue, eventually I wouldn't be able to abandon Sara one night, and someone would die because of it. Or worse, I would, and something would get to Sara while I was gone.

It was the classic superhero dilemma, except I'm not a superhero. I'm no cape-wearing super-speedy mensch who would benefit from the karmic balance of having saved the world. I was simply Ze'ev Kaplan, a Jew who tried to do everything in my power to do the right thing in bad situations. Life had been more dangerous than usual this year, though; I didn't normally have to deal with ghouls hunting me for sport or with murderous cults. The cult was all but dealt with now, even those last two murderous motherfuckers were going to get caught and go to prison. But what about the ghouls? I still had to contend with the bullshit that Grin was sending me.

Thinking of Grin and the chores he had sent me earlier reminded me that I was stalling on checking my phone. I sighed and pulled the device out of my pocket before swiping it on.

76 missed calls.

I blinked at the screen. That was a lot. That was more than Sara being pissed or anything reasonable. That was an emergency. My heart racing, I started swiping through the call history.

Nearly every single call was from Alex Barman, the cop who I had used to nail Basken to the wall. Relatively few voicemails, but so many calls. I worried that I had set him in the path of violence or cult retaliation. Hesitantly, I pushed play on the first message.

"Zev, it's Alex. I need a favor, call me as soon as you get this."

"Zev, come on. Hey, maybe you didn't get my last call. I need some help, man, please, it's serious."

"Zev, Goddamnit! Fucking call me back! I need help, please."
My heart sank. Each message sounded more and more distraught, more panicked. I considered skipping the rest of the calls and just calling him back, but I was terrified to find out what I was walking into.

"Zev, look, I know your recovering from what happened, I get it, but I need help. My daughter is missing, Zev. Haley is missing, and I need help. I know you were, you said you were, Israeli special forces, and please ... please ..."
My heart ached through my chest. It felt like a physical blow that knocked me onto my ass. I found the curb and sat down heavily on the concrete, staring at the phone in silence. That was the last call, but I could see I had many unread emails. I flicked my thumb across the icon, afraid of where this path would lead. There it was, the first email, condolences to the Barman family ... service times, Shivah hours ... I glanced at my watch. It was too late now, I would need to wait, maybe try to sleep, though I doubted sleep would come. There are many uncomfortable things one

must do as an adult, and as a friend. But this was a culmination of fears, this could be my fault, and I couldn't avoid Alex just for the sake of my comfort. I had to make Shivah. I walked back to my house. I couldn't make this right, but I could do my best to share in the despair.

✡

I drove to the Barmans' in the morning. I wasn't sure what to do, so I sat in the car for several minutes. In the seat next to me was a box of pastries from Swedish Hill Bakery, nothing special, but when making Shivah, it's encouraged to help provide for the mourning family. I hadn't made Shivah too many times in the past, but it was always an awkward visit. I never knew what to say to a family mourning a loss, despite having lost my own father and childhood friend. Death never became less awkward. This death in particular had added discomfort. Alex had reached out for my help, and I had not been there.

I swallowed my discomfort, grabbed the pastries, and headed up the walkway to knock on the door lightly. Part of me prayed they wouldn't be home. They were, of course. A woman answered, her ringlet black hair tied out of her face. She was drawn, and her eyes were puffy, as though she had been crying for the last week without any break from the pain. I supposed that was probably the case. I lifted the box in front of me like a tribute offered on the ancient alter of the temple. She took in my kippah, tallit katan and decided I must be from the synagogue, because she stepped aside to let me enter. It was dark inside, the light mostly coming from the early morning sun filtering through the windows.

"I am so sorry for your loss." I kept my voice

down, aware that other people in the house could still be asleep. The woman, Alex's wife, I assumed, took the box of pastries from me and nodded.

"I'm sorry, you're ..."

"Ze'ev, uh, Zev Kaplan. I attend the same shul. I was heartbroken to hear ..." I trailed off, feeling the awkwardness.

"Yeah, we all are, Zev." She stepped away and put the box I had brought in the kitchen before turning to me and crossing her arms over her stomach. I recognized the gesture as the type a person did when they were trying to hold their emotions in check, as though you could physically hold grief in place. "I'm Hayley's mom, I was ..." she started to correct herself, but broke off, controlling her emotions as best she could.

I stayed silent, unable to add anything to help. I remembered that her name was Sandra from the email that had been sent out. We stood in silence for a moment, her waiting and me searching for some way to supply the comfort I was supposedly here for.

"I'm sorry ..."

"Sorry, sorry sorry sorry sorry sorry, I am so fucking sick of sorry. No, I'm sorry, but why do you and everyone else keep saying that? Do you think I care about you being sorry? Do you think it makes any difference to me at all?" Her eyes were hard glints of anger in the low light.

I nodded.

"Because we don't know what else to say, Sandra. There's nothing any of us can say, so we fumble with words we've been given ... I'm not an orator or a rabbi or ... I'm just someone who knows Alex and who wishes I could help in any way." The words tumbled out nearly unbidden as I tried to justify my presence, not just to her but to myself.

Her eyes softened a little as she looked down. I could hear the soft sobs coming from her, and my instinct was to move and hold her, to comfort her, but I was a stranger. I was a stranger in her home who brought her some apple turnovers as a consolation prize for losing her daughter. Instead, I stood there doing my best to look non-judgmental.

"Zev?"

Alex's voice almost made me jump in the near silence of the darkened home. For a moment, Alex looked like he was going to storm across the room and hit me. Maybe he would, maybe I deserved it. Instead, he walked to his wife and wrapped his arms around her, rocking her gently. He kissed the side of her head in a display of affection that, for some reason, made my heart ache all the more.

"Would you like some coffee," he asked me, though the tone made it obvious it wasn't actually a question.

"I don't want to intrude." I took a step towards the door, but his look, something between rage and sorrow, made me stop, and I nodded. "Okay, I can have some coffee," I agreed.

Sandra disappeared into the kitchen as Alex approached me.

"I called."

"I saw. I mean, I saw last night. My phone was broken. I didn't see I had any missed calls until ..." I let the sentence trail off, frustrated at how easy lying came to me.

But Alex was nodding, he believed me. He gestured to the couch and sat in a nearby rocking chair. His hands moved across the wood armrests.

"My mother gave me this after Hayley was born, same rocking chair she got when I was born ..." He looked up at me. "I need to find who did this."

I met his eyes, searching for some explanation of what he meant. I could put the pieces together and guess that someone had kidnapped and hurt Hayley, but my information was limited to the sporadic voicemails and the email sent to the congregation.

"As a police officer, don't you have those tools?" I asked, but was rewarded by him almost violently shaking his head.

"No, not only do I not have the tools, the precinct is keeping me out of the investigation." He looked off into the distance, clear frustration etched across his features. "You're a private investigator, right? A PI?"

"Uh, not exactly. I just have a job that has me wrapped up in things once in a while. But why do you want a PI?"

"You investigate things." He pressed.

"I ... well, sort of, but I'm not ... not these sort of things, Alex."

"You could. You could investigate this sort of thing." He was determined.

I could see it on his face that he was reaching out not just for a friend but for someone to just say they would help him. But I didn't, I didn't look into human crimes unless they were supernatural in nature. This was so far outside my bailiwick as an exorcist that it felt alien and more frightening than dealing with a rampaging aluca.

"And you're former special services."

I wish I hadn't told him that. I wish I hadn't been forced to play that card to stay out of jail, but what was done was done. I finally nodded. There was no use denying the past, and there was no point pretending I didn't know what he was saying or asking of me.

"I can see if I can find anything, Alex, but ... if I did, it may not be admissible in court." I watched his face darken; he had no intention of taking it to court. Maybe that's why he wanted me, to find the killer before his precinct did so that he could administer a father's justice. Would I do any different? Could I empower a good man to become a murderer?

"I just want to stop them before they hurt any more kids, Ze'ev."

I nodded; the world was never black and white, it was never clear or clean. But if faced with a decision between doing nothing and stopping a child murderer, I would rather answer to the Accuser than to myself.

Alex rose and grabbed a manila folder off the mantle above his fireplace, offering it to me before sitting back down. Sandra came out of the kitchen with a cup of coffee. Her eyes narrowed a little at the sight of the folder as I took it and flipped it open and then immediately closed it again.

"You shouldn't have this."

"It's copies. The detective actually working the case has everything in there." Alex shrugged.

"That isn't … that's only partially what I mean, Alex. Do you think having these pictures in your home is healthy?!"

"That's what I've been telling him," Sandra said as she set my coffee down in front of me. "But he keeps insisting he knows someone who *will* help. Is that you?"

"Has he offered the folder to anyone else?" I asked in return, irritated that I was the villain here, corrupting her husband in an already heartbreakingly tragic moment in their lives. "I'll see what I can do," I finally muttered under her dragon-like gaze.

"What you can do? You can't do anything. Finding out who did this isn't going to bring Hayley back, and I think you should leave it to professionals."

At least she and I agreed on something here. I

stayed silent, unsure what to say. Alex looked equally uncomfortable, like he had been caught looking at pornography on the family desktop.

Finally, he shook his head and rose from the rocking chair. "Zev is just another pair of eyes. Like I told him, I don't want this to happen to anyone else."

"I'll do everything I can," I answered, rising as well, taking it as an invitation to beat a hasty retreat, my coffee untouched. I wanted to get out from under Sandra's angry eyes, but to be honest, I found Alex's hope just as oppressive. He put his faith in me, while his wife was laying the full cruelty of the situation at my feet in that moment. I offered my hand to Alex, and after shaking it, I gave Sandra my best apologetic smile, which was probably more awkward than it was comforting, and left as quickly as I could, the manila folder tucked under my arm.

Chapter 3

I had crashed my car during my showdown with Basken. I had hoped it would be salvageable, but in the end, I had to say goodbye to my trusty steed. I cared less about the actual vehicle than I did the reintroduction of a car payment into my life, but there was no real avoiding it. I had put in an expense request, seeing as I had wrecked the old car in the line of duty, but so far, the Beit Din didn't seem too keen on expensing a 2018 Dodge Challenger. I wonder why.

There were some benefits to my new car; the AC and heater actually worked, which was nice, and it had a Bluetooth stereo that connected to my phone. I turned everything on and left the Barmans' house as quickly as I could and went through a drive-through at a taco joint to get some coffee I could actually drink and a couple of tacos. To tell the truth, I was more used to eating in my car than not these days. I pulled into a space in the parking lot to eat while I looked over the information in the folder.

Again, I was treated to the full Strumpfsy images of the remains of Hayley. I wanted to look away, my brain still hurt from watching Kristine die, but

I couldn't. I forced myself to look. She had been ripped apart. The body was a horrifying mess, a tangle of limbs bent the wrong way and huge gobs of flesh and meat just missing. She was a child who had been savaged. Only her face remained untouched. Her neck was broken, the head lolled at an unnatural angle with her eyes, bloodshot and milky, staring up into the camera and my soul. I turned the picture over, hiding the image. I had seen plenty of death and undeath, but I couldn't look a dead girl in the eyes without feeling the crushing weight of mortality and the cruelty that was still alive in the world no matter how hard I worked to whittle it down.

Behind the photos were reports: police reports, missing person reports filed by the parents, copies of evidence reports. It was a copious amount of paperwork, but what I was most interested in at that moment was the coroner's report. In the pictures, it looked like the ten-year-old girl had been torn apart and tossed around like a rag doll. I blew on my coffee, my eyes looking over the paperwork. It was worse than I had imagined. The damage I had seen in the picture—the rips and tears and broken bones—had all happened ante-mortem. There were no drugs found in her system, no signs of sexual violence. I thanked HaShem for the smallest blessings in what was turning into a maelstrom of terror. No food in her stomach either, she had been starved of food and water in the days leading up to her violent death. This was torture, plain and simple. I set the paper aside for a moment. Looked at the breakfast taco I had bought. I didn't want to eat.

But I needed to. I had to get food in my stomach or I wouldn't be able to think straight. I glanced at the folder next to me as I unwrapped my breakfast and added salsa. Chewing on my first bite, I thought about the ramifications of the torture. When a child is kidnapped, it's almost always someone close to the family. Usually it's someone who either feels they should be the child's caretaker or a reprehensible predator. When a child was taken, we always assumed there was some perversion at work, something horrific. But the absence of that with the presence of so much violence baffled every ounce of forensic and criminology profiling that my time watching crime procedurals had given me. I flipped through the pages with my free hand, pausing when the word *inconclusive* caught my eye.

Pulling the evidence report out from the stack of paper, I looked it over. Hair and saliva were found all over the body, which made sense, it looked like some wild animal had gotten a hold of her or someone had let their dog attack her. I shuddered at the thought of someone training an animal to kill using a child. But the tests on the hair were inconclusive, it wasn't canine, similar but not really. From reading the attached comments, it sounded like the analysts were stumped.

There is always a danger when you look at something of trying to fit it into your world view. When what you have is an exorcist's hammer, everything looks like a monstrous nail to be smashed. Maybe this was my kind of work after all. I shoved the papers back into the folder and pulled out of the parking lot. Time to go to the lab and let Rivkah know we weren't done burning the midnight oil just yet.

✡

Rivkah and I were about as different as could be. I had grown up in North Texas and spent a lot of time in the Chasidic communities; because of that,

I tended towards more traditional outfits like dark suits. I didn't have any piercings or tattoos. Most people who saw me probably assumed I was ultra-orthodox because I had the kitan tallit and kipah on. Though the truth was that most Haradim would say I wasn't religious at all because I wasn't strict enough in my observance.

Rivkah was a child of the metal scene from California and had a swirl of tattoos in blacks and reds painting evil looking images and hypersexual imagery across most of her body. Her half-shorn hair was rarely a natural color, the short loose curls going from black to purple or green, depending on her mood and the seasons. She had more piercings in her ears than most of the women in my family combined, not to mention the couple in her eyebrow, the nose stud, lip, and tongue. She was a petite woman in height, but had the sort of curves that made people stop and stare. I sometimes thought her tattoos and piercings were a warning system, warning predators to keep away from her. With her looks, she would have had to get real tough, real fast.

She was on the phone when I opened the door to our little warehouse/workshop/laboratory. She was speaking in fast Hebrew, which was rare. Very rare. When she had first started joined the Beit Din and started working for me, she had essentially just known her prayers, but I always insisted that she learn to be fluent. It garnered more respect from our bosses, and it gave us the ability to talk about our work in public, since most people couldn't speak the language.

"No, wait, Rabbi Schulman, he just walked in ... No, I don't know, he literally just walked in ... I told you that his phone was haunted!" She was animated, and her bright long hoodie swirled like a cloak every time she turned.

I knew the feeling, Nathan could be a pain in the ass. It sometimes felt like he was attempting to be irritating. I offered her a kind smile. She snarled silently at me. I wasn't sure if it was supposed to be intimidating, it just looked adorable.

"Here!" She shouted, thrusting the phone at me.

I stared at it in her out-thrust had a moment like it was a demon with teeth that would take my hand off. Her pouty face and fierce dark eyes lined green eyeliner and black shadow convinced me that not taking the phone would both make her sad and make her hurt me. I smiled and took the phone, steeling myself before hitting speaker-phone and answering.

"Shalom, Nathan."

"You don't ignore my calls, Ze'ev." His voice was curt, and he spoke in the heavily-accented Hebrew of the Chasidim, without any warmth. It was typical of Nathan, but it hadn't always been. At one point, we had been friends; he had been caring, insightful, and funny. I wondered what happened to that Nathan.

"I was chasing down the last of that cult and the necromancers. You can see it on the news here in Texas."

There was a pause, and I heard some clicking as Nathan searched through google. I waited patiently, moving through our little workspace towards my desk so I could sit and look at the various papers and mail that had accumulated while I was gone.

"Is that the last of them?"

"From what we've been able to find, they had a statue to some goddess, I think. It came alive and ..." I trailed off. Talking calmly about the woman's death felt wrong. I didn't feel calm, I felt angry and powerless. *"Anyway, that's where I've been. I'll send in my final report, and since that cult is gone now, I should be able to start carrying my normal phone with*

me again."

"I'm glad to hear that they're going to pay for their crimes, and that you are safe, but that isn't why I'm calling, actually."

My heart sank.

"No, Nathan, no, you can't give me another job right now. I've been on this for months. I need a break, and I'm helping out a friend with something heavy ..."

"I'm sorry that things are hard, but the world doesn't wait for us, Ze'ev. Do you remember the Cohens from Memphis? Their daughter, Sandy?" Nathan asked it very quickly; he knew I wasn't going to like where this was leading.

"Yeah, that exorcism kicked off all of this. What's happened?" When a kid, especially one in the midst of puberty, had a brush with the supernatural, something tended to stick. You became a magnet for more and more of that sort of interaction. Not always, but usually. That's what had happened with me. A dybbuk and a possession had led to more and more dangerous confrontations with supernatural entities, and eventually, I had been recruited and trained by the Beit Din. Hopefully, nothing too bad happened to Sandy. It was usually a slow rise to dangerous entities. Usually.

"Ah, happened, nothing has happened yet, but the family has had visitors ... Entities gathering outside their home, following them at night, there one moment then gone the next. Typical Sheydim haunting."

Typical Sheydim haunting was a load of shit; there was no such thing as a typical Sheydim haunting. And really, haunting was the wrong word. They didn't haunt, they stalked. They weren't ghosts or dybbuks, they were intelligent, usually ancient beings that always had some greater agenda in mind. Even the lesser Sheydim, like Baladan, who I had met on a handful of occasions, were dangerous.

34

"*Uh huh,*" I answered, waiting for the other shoe to drop.

"*You're going to take her in, help train her to protect herself, and get her re—*"

"*No.*"

"*No?*"

"*No, Nathan, I am absolutely not going to bring a child into my life. Are you insane? Do you know what sort of gymnastics I would have to pull with people here to explain the sudden presence of a child?*"

"*Claim she is your niece.*"

"*Most people know my sisters, Nathan! You know my sisters!*" I was shouting. My sisters weren't Beit Din, though both Kim and Sammy were some of the few who knew about it, but as I mentioned earlier, they weren't the sort who would have kids. Sammy might adopt one day, but she was mostly business; business and women were the only things she had much time for these days.

"*This isn't a request, Ze'ev.*"

"*No, it's insane is what it is. Who am I to take care of a child?*"

"*You're the best option!*" Now Nathan was shouting too. We really brought out the best in one another.

"*Ah! You ARE insane then!*" I felt triumphant that he would be caught in his disdain for me and the necessity of using me.

"*Ze'ev.*" He stopped shouting, he sounded tired. "*Could we send her somewhere else? Yes. And she'll be even farther from home and her parents. She's already scared. She spends the school year in Austin with you, she goes to school, you teach her in the evenings while protecting her from the things her family can't. Then in the summer, she goes back to stay with her family. Maybe she doesn't need more than that, but she needs help, and no one understands that loneliness better than you.*"

That was unfair. It was a low blow. I sat heavily in my desk chair and set the phone on the desk, covering my face with my hands. I was so tired. Tired of danger, tired of all the lies, and this would just be more lies added to the heap. Rivkah touched my shoulder.

"She can stay with me," she said with a small smile. "I helped raise my niece, and I always wanted a little sister, so, she can stay with me, and you can just be professor. Everyone wins. The family would probably be more comfortable with their daughter staying with a woman anyway, right?"

I reached up and squeezed her hand before addressing the phone again. *"Have them contact me, Nathan. We'll figure out logistics from there, but I'm counting on you to grease any wheels and deal with red tape and paperwork. I refuse to do that."*

"What else is new?" He returned to his normal grumpy self, and me to my smart-ass self. All was right in the world.

Except it wasn't. I needed to find a killer and protect Sandy from both the Sheydim and from the Beit Din.

"Goodbye, Nathan." I hung up before he could respond and gave Rivkah a long suffering look. "No rest for the righteous." I pulled the manila folder out of my coat. "Now, sit; I have to go over this with you, and it isn't pleasant."

Chapter 4

When all was said and done, we had a plan for Sandy. She would take the Greyhound bus down to Austin, where I would get her and start getting her situated in what would be her new lifestyle. I felt sorry for the girl, a teenage girl deserved to be around friends, going to the movies and fooling around in the back of the theater, all the banal shit that teenagers got into. The things that we left behind as adults. But instead, she would be stuck in a Jewish private school in the morning and dealing with the wide world of mystical inanity in the evening.

Rivkah and I discussed it whenever we needed a break from looking over the paperwork related to Hayley's death. Suddenly, the forced presence of a ward was the least intrusive and unpleasant aspect life was throwing at me right now. Rivkah would do everything she could to keep Sandy's life intact, meaning she was going to become a chauffeur for a teenager. I also resolved to teach her self-defense and shooting. Whether or not the Beit Din wormed its fingers into her life, she would need to be able to watch after herself. She wouldn't need to be a damsel when she could be the knight.

Luckily for me, I had trained someone before. I glanced past the stack of papers on the table between me at Rivkah, the longer half of her hair hung over her face. She was easily smarter than I would ever be, and she had been a fantastic student. My own hangups had put stumbling blocks in my way as I dealt with the attractive and tattooed woman. But she had also been my age and curious about the supernatural world. Would Sandy be as curious? Would these things come naturally to her, or would she be indifferent about this new subject she was being forced to learn? Back in Memphis, she had been curious, she had finished prayers and wanted to be involved. I had chalked it up to her being a naturally curious teen at the time. But now I wondered how curious she had been. Had she attempted magic? Had she brought the attention of the Sheydim down on herself?

"Can I help you?" Rivkah asked, one pierced eyebrow cocked up at me.

I realized that while my mind had wandered, my eyes had not, and I had been sitting and staring at Rivkah for probably a few minutes now.

"I'm not all that bad of a teacher, am I?" I asked, leaning back and rubbing my eyes.

"What do you mean?"

"Well, you turned out all right, yeah?"

"What makes you say that?" she returned. She was getting better at this. Answering questions with questions was a wonderful skill because it made it sound like you were taking your ego out of the equation, it softened statements. Better, but not perfect; she wasn't answering.

"Why wouldn't I say that?" I questioned.

"Would you say that if I hadn't stayed on helping you with ... well everything?"

"Would you stay and help if I had been a bad teacher?"

"I suppose not," she conceded. "Besides, I think according to the Beit Din, I'm still your student, aren't I?" Again with the eyebrow.

I nodded, though I was thinking about the way her piercing accented facial expressions and made her look more expressive, like the way her eye makeup made her eyes look even larger.

"And you will be until someone calls me on it. When you graduate, they send you off to do this on your own. You don't need that, but I will always need you." She blushed. "Your help, I mean," I corrected quickly.

I don't think Rivkah felt the tension I did. To her, I was a teacher, a friend, and a boss. To me, she was a student, a friend, and an assistant. Any thoughts I had about her that were anything other than pure were my problem to sort out. But I always felt guilty. I was not a single man, and every time I thought about another woman as being attractive, I felt that twinge of guilt, like my thoughts were a betrayal. I covered my thoughts with a smile.

"If you get tired of me and want to strike out on your own, you just tell me, and I'll write my approval and letter of recommendation to the Beit Din that minute," I said.

She nodded thoughtfully at that. "Even if it means losing your assistant?"

"Who am I to keep you from what you want?" I asked.

My phone let out the low drone of a call, interrupting what was likely to be another bout of questions. I turned it over and looked at the screen: a text from Alex Barman.

Turn on the local news.

I hated that. You never got a text or call that said *turn on the news* and saw a fluff piece about a capybara that befriended a kangaroo. It was always a disaster, a shoot-out, some new display of human cruelty. I stood and moved over to the lone TV we had in the office and flipped it on, turning channels until I hit a news program. I figured out immediately why Alex had wanted me to tune in.

It had happened again. Another missing child.

The camera panned over the family and focused on the door where a father stood in stoic despair, trying to give a statement to the police. Above his shoulder, I saw a mezuzah. Not just another child, another Jewish child missing. This wasn't just some predator, this was a predator that was seeking out the youth of my community. I didn't recognize the Lekowitz family, but I would be willing to bet that this family also attended Beth Israel like Alex. It was either another member of the synagogue or it was someone who watched the synagogue.

"Zev?"

I jumped before turning to face Rivkah, so absorbed in my thoughts that I had forgotten I wasn't alone.

"We're going to stop this guy, right?" she asked.

I looked back at the TV. My fists were clenched so tight that I thought my skin might rip. I nodded, unable to bring myself to talk, not trusting the words to come without screaming in rage and sorrow.

I haven't watched a lot of crime procedurals, and neither Rivkah nor I were forensic specialists; but I had some skill with magic and divination, and Rivkah was pretty much the smartest person in any room. We had also gotten pretty good at tracking people while cleaning up Basken's cult. We had a few more threads to pull on at that point, though. At the moment, I was floundering in the dark. I handed the evidence report to Rivkah. In another life, before she had joined me, she had been a chemist with more than a smattering of biology under her wing. If anyone could crack the lab results, it would be her. In the meantime, I cleared off the table and placed a large roadmap of Austin there. In red marker, I drew large circles around the neighborhoods where the attacks had happened.

This, in and of itself, didn't give me all that much information. After just a little bit of searching, I had found that they were both indeed members of Congregation Beth Israel. I circled the synagogue in blue and then stared at the map, willing it to just give me the answers without me doing anything. It didn't. I could try getting in touch with Anthony again, the albino empath who helped me beat Basken, but I didn't have any answers for him yet, and I knew that would be the first thing on his mind. Besides, I had more information when I went after Basken—I knew his voice, I knew his people, his intention. I didn't know shit about this killer.

"Hey, Zev?" Rivkah called from her own desk, which was bigger than mine and laden with computers, scientific equipment, and research books. She would—as soon as I actually let her go—become possibly the greatest mystical researcher the Beit Din had ever possessed.

I walked over and stared at the computer screen she was showing me. It had a lot of chemical compounds and formulae on it, and the second screen looked like something from the Ancestry DNA testing website. I nodded as it if meant anything to me. She stared at me, probably wondering who I was trying to fool.

"Okay, look, here's what I did. First, I entered all the data from the tests the police ran. I took the results from the saliva and the results from the hair, and I looked at them separately and together. The police thought they were from two different sources, but I don't think so ..." She clicked and clacked a moment, and the various numbers and colored lines moved. I didn't bother pretending to see the significance this time. "I think they're from the same animal or person ... thing."

"You're suggesting that one animal has different DNA and chemicals in its hair than in its saliva? I didn't think that's how DNA worked."

"It isn't—it shouldn't be anyway—but look at this; lets treat it like a mathematical equation."

"Oh, my favorite," I teased.

"Shut up, professor. Just, follow me here. I take out the markers that would typically be found in human DNA." She clicked a few keys, and the image shifted slightly. "We are left with almost pure canine DNA, wolf specifically; and the saliva, while most of these compounds could be found in any human's mouth, some are things I would expect in canine, right?" She was excited; I knew where she was connecting the dots.

"Rivka, the last known werewolf was killed by the Baal Shem Tov nearly three hundred years ago, and even that's just a legend.

"Does that matter? Does it matter when it was last seen by the community at large?"

"No," I admitted, staring at the work she had done. I had no idea how to address a werewolf. There were almost as many legends surrounding the idea of shape shifters as there were cultures in the world. "But it doesn't make our job any easier knowing that."

"It could if we could get a hair sample ..." Rivkah suggested.

"As true as that is, how the hell ..." I sighed. Alex would get it for me, he would do anything I asked him to right now, but it was taking advantage of his despair. "Okay, I'll see what I can do; but look, even if we get the hair, even if your theory is right, we have a lot of work to do and not much time to do it in."

Rivkah nodded and turned back to her computer while I headed out the door to call Alex. In the story, the werewolf was a charcoal burner who was possessed by evil spirits. He transformed into a horrifying beast that reeked. In some stories, he killed children; in others, he only attacked them before being run off by them. Some stories told of the Baal Shem Tov going into the forest and praying, killing the werewolf with sheer holiness. In others, he crushed the thing's head with a cudgel, cut out its heart, and buried the still beating organ. Both seemed dangerous prospects. Once the thing was dead, it assumed a human shape, and then ... well then there would be a corpse and an investigation. I don't actually enjoy being on the wrong side of the law.

I flicked my phone on to call Alex and saw I had yet another missed text, this one from Sara. Fantastic.

Dinner? Or have you pretty much decided you're done with the whole being in a relationship thing?

I winced. Sara, I loved Sara, but this work had taken over my life more than usual. With the stakeouts and not having my phone with me most the time, I was definitely skating on thin ice with her. I sent a quick text back, saying dinner sounded great and that I would make it up to her and that I loved her. Of course, all I got back was a 'k'. Great. Just one more thing to deal with. Maybe I was avoiding Sara because every time I saw her lately, we were bickering, fighting, and, of course, I couldn't honestly answer any of her questions, and so I lied. I lied and I was sure she could sense that.

I shoved my phone back in my pocket. I needed to go to the store and get stuff to make dinner. That, at least, was a concrete goal I could do without fucking everything up too much.

Chapter 5

I got a hold of Alex while leaving the store, and he agreed to get a hair sample for us. I didn't ask how he would steal evidence from a case he wasn't supposed to be working, and he didn't offer details. That suited me fine. He would bring the hair sample by my lab sometime after I picked Sandy up from the Greyhound station. It was going to be a busy one. I was never good at juggling too many balls at once. One reason I stayed with the Beit Din maybe, they only ever assigned one thing to me at a time, or usually did anyway. With Sandy in the picture, who knew what was going to happen; they would probably look for more excuses to throw projects my way in order to train the girl.

I could train her in a few different ways—spell work, esoteric philosophy, and magical theory. Back in the old days, you had to be over 30, married, male, and well versed in Torah, Talmud, and the Mishnah before anyone would even think of letting you study Kabbalah, and with good reason. Diving into esoteric thought unprepared could lead to a mindset that was dangerous. It could turn a person into an egomaniac or a dangerous nihilist … or simply drive a person insane.

But sometime around the late 19th and early 20th century, things got bad. I blamed the surge in seances and dime-store mystics. They may have been full of shit, but the intention was there, the desire, and it called the dead like the brightest beacon you could imagine. Dybbuk and other inhuman aberration activity skyrocketed. A world in which only a few exorcists or monster hunters existed meant soon there would be none. It also meant more young children and teens were encountering the supernatural, being marked by them, and being forced into my world.

I didn't want to force Sandy down the path I walked; not many people were suited for it. Being an exorcist wasn't that bad. Dybbukim tended to not be aggressive or dangerous, and when they were dangerous, they were really only as dangerous as any other human being. There were exceptions. The thing in her mirror, for instance. It had tried to reach out with no body and drag me to Sheol. But that was an outlier.

But being a monster hunter, hunting the other things that went bump in the night, that was different. That was always dangerous. Most of them were intelligent, crafty, and had no qualms about killing a person. It was rarer in the modern era. But it wasn't rare enough for me. I had been trained up and tasked with it due to my time in the military, something I would do my best to steer Sandy away from. Encountering monsters in a warzone was just about the worst experience anyone can come against.

My train of thought on various methods of teaching a teenager ancient wisdom for busting ghosts was interrupted by the sudden glare of red and blue lights. Fuck me. I pulled over into a small neighborhood and to the side of the road. I texted Sara to let her know I was getting pulled over so would be a little later that I originally thought. I wasn't sure why I was being pulled over. I doubted I had been speeding, but sometimes that did get away from me. I watched the cop walking over to my door. Police were always a wild card. Sometimes they would tell me all about how they supported Israel and how their church prayed for the Jews. Sometimes they were conspiracy theorists who thought that I somehow ruled the world from my little car. My least favorite joke was asking to search my trunk for gold bars.

This cop looked like a stereotype, like someone asked a casting agent to grab the person who looked the most like a policeman, threw him in a too tight uniform, and yelled action. He had greased back hair and huge mirrored aviators above a bushy handlebar mustache and a too wide smile. I hated that smile. That smile wasn't saying he was friendly, it was saying he loved what he was doing. It said that pulling me over was probably one of the highlights of his day. I groaned a little, grabbing my ID and insurance and tossing them on the dashboard before I rolled down my window.

He approached and then stood there, presumably looking down at me, taking in the suit, the kippah, everything about me that screamed *Jew*. His smile widened, showing off even more teeth. Teeth that frankly looked too numerous and too sharp anyway.

"Evening, officer, " I offered.

"It is indeed, buddy, it is indeed!" he returned, almost in a sing song tone.

I stared, unsure how to respond to his answer or his tone.

"Name?"

I glanced at my paperwork sitting on the dashboard, wondering when he would ask for that. Not right now was apparently the answer. I looked back up at the cop. He was still grinning from ear to ear. There was something unnatural about him, something that set me on edge.

"Ze'ev Kaplan."

"Ze'ev." He said my name like he was tasting it, seeing how it felt in his mouth. "Kinda unusual name, ain't it? Some kind of Jewish name, I'm guessing." He set his hand down on my car door so that his fingers curled over the open window; they had four joints each curling in to grip the door. This thing wasn't human. His name badge said Stevens.

"Just mine, I guess, just a Jewish name ..." I slowly reached forward towards the gear shift, keeping my eyes on my reflection in his glasses. He gave a slight shake of his head. A warning. "What can I do for you ... *officer*?"

"Your registration is expired there, Ze'ev." His gaze didn't waver in the least. "I just thought I would stop you, Ze'ev, and see why you would drive around with expired registration, Ze'ev." He turned my name into a threat, a I-know-who-you-are.

I didn't know who he was or what he was or why he was stopping me. But the fact was, I was marked by my experiences, a beacon for things like this. It could just be a random happenstance, but I doubted that.

"You see, Ze'ev," he continued, "I know that you're working with a mutual acquaintance. It's a small world, isn't it, Ze'ev? It's a small damn world. Now I think what your doing is great, Ze'ev, right? But see, there are others who don't, who won't. Who think what your doing is shit, Ze'ev. And if they were to notice your registration is out of date, Ze'ev ..." He leaned back and shook his head as though what would happen didn't bear speaking aloud.

"You're from the ..." I started.

"Austin Police Department," he finished, his grin growing in size and menace with each word.

"Court," I finished for myself, watching his face carefully. I hated that I couldn't see the thing's eyes, that his fingers were so close to me, that he was standing above me, and that I was trapped in a car, buckled in, while he had the full range of motion. My hand was on the shift. I could drop into drive and hit the gas, but could I do it faster than this thing could rip out my throat?

"I'm not a messenger sent by anyone. This is independent work, Ze'ev." He reached up with the hand not on my door and removed his glasses. Empty sockets stared back at me. Something with too many eyes and legs shifted inside the socket. My stomach turned. "A concerned on-looker, watching what's going to become a pile-up." On the last word, the thing inside his socket squirmed out. It looked like a millipede with a humanoid face. Each of its legs ended in a serrated blade. It crawled over the cop's face and down his chin and shoulder, working its way down his arm. Towards me.

I felt almost frozen. While the few Sheydim I had met had been fairly easy going, Baladan had found me in the realm of dreams and warned me about getting involved in Sheydim politics. I occasionally had dealt with Sheydim in my work. The truth was that Sheydim were probably the most dangerous creatures in existence until you got to celestial beings. Immortal, possessing strange powers, and possessing the entire spectrum of human emotion, along with human capability for cold cruelty. Some Sheydim were simply strong, others rivaled angels with their powers.

This one brought nightmare visions of John Carpenter's Thing, all squirming flesh and mandibles clashing with human features that were as menacing as they were unsettling. Then the crawling thing spoke, its voice a deep baritone. "Keep your friends close, boy, but take care to realize who your enemies are."

I couldn't handle that. I slammed the car into drive and stomped the gas. I half expected the car not to move, that this Sheyd cop would just lift the vehicle and his eye-worm-thing would reach me and burrow into my skull. Instead, he let go, and I screeched down the street. Looking in my rearview, certain he would be chasing, I was treated to a view of him replacing his sunglasses and waving. I wasn't hungry anymore. All I wanted to do was get back to the lab and see if I could dig up anything on the creature that had just stopped me. But I couldn't. Part of maintaining a secret life is knowing when you have to make a show at being normal.

Once the Sheyd was out of sight, I slowed down, waiting for my heart to do the same, and continued on my way to Sara's house.

Sara was in a mood. I couldn't blame her. I had been unresponsive and absent for months now, and frankly, things had been strained since I had been laid up in the hospital. We were in the kitchen silently cooking together. Sara was one of the kindest and most generous people I had ever met; she wasn't religious, but she was good. Even when she wasn't at work saving lives, she was doing charity work. It was probably the only reason she hadn't dumped me. She was as busy as I was. She moved around the kitchen like an angel, an extremely fit and sexy angel. Or maybe a figure skater would be a more apt and less blasphemous phrase. She was graceful, moving naturally between shelves and the stove and practically dancing over her slobbering mess of a dog, Toof. I enjoyed the way her body moved. I could usually admire her without feeling sleazy or gross. But tonight, my mind was torn between the guilt of putting her through so much and the terror that my life was about to be flooded with inhuman monsters … again.

Still, even though the encounter with the *cop* had been terrifying, it hadn't actually been violent—Basken's cultists had tried to kill me immediately. So maybe I was over reacting. While the Sheydim could be humanly cruel, they also had the same capacity for kindness and goodness. I shook the thoughts from my head, desperate to be in the moment. Sara was grabbing plates from the shelves, and her small cotton shorts were riding up her legs, giving me a fantastic view of her butt. That could help.

"Enjoying the view?" Sara asked. She was still on her tip-toes, but was no longer reaching for plates; instead she stuck out her butt and wiggled it.

"Very much so," I answered, setting down the spoon I had been using to stir dinner. "Very much." I pressed into her. Feeling her firm roundness against me always ignited an almost feral level of lust in me. I wrapped my arms around her waist and gave a little shake, letting her feel my body's reaction to her.

She smiled, pulling away just enough to turn full in my arms, and pressed her face close to mine. I could smell her vanilla lotion and feel the shift of her muscles beneath her taut skin. Her lips grazed mine for a moment before I felt her teeth tugging on my lips, pulling a low growl of need from me. I wanted to forget dinner. I wanted to forget everything else but Sara. She was all I needed, and I needed her badly. It had been weeks since we had been intimate. I cupped her ass and lifted her onto the counter, not breaking the kiss we had going. Without looking, I could feel her shifting her clothes, lifting her butt so she could push her shorts down her legs. I reached down to undo my own pants when she pulled away.

"I think you need an appetizer before dinner, baby." She wrapped her hands around the back of my neck and guided me down.

I wasn't one to argue with a before dinner snack and buried my face in her. My hands roamed her thighs and ass as I eagerly explored her with my tongue. Her fingers scratched through my scalp and moved under my collar to scratch at my shoulders and back. The world of Sheydim and Dybbukim fell away. Worries, werewolves, wards, and cultists evaporated in the maelstrom of Sara's moans.

It wasn't until after dinner that the bliss from my appetizer drained away from us both. I suggested we watch a movie, and Sara rolled her eyes. She suggested maybe instead we do something together.

"How is it not together?"

"How is it? We aren't talking or interacting while watching a movie, we're just sitting there."

"Together," I pressed.

"Occupying the same space isn't the same as spending time together, Zev." She had me there. But I was at a loss. The truth was I was hoping to mostly ignore the movie and move on to the main course I had started earlier. Apparently, Sara wasn't on the same page. "I mean, holy shit, Zev, we've barely seen each other in weeks, and when we finally do, you want to watch ... what? Some mindless action film?" She sighed.

"No, I just thought it would be something that we could relax and unwind to. Mindless is good for that, you don't have to pay attention." I spent so much time with my mind so busy, so filled with worry and thought, that the balm of mindless media was somewhat soothing.

"I want you paying attention, Zev. I want you paying attention to me!" There was a storm of raging frustration on her face, an emotional roller coaster that matched the anxiety I was feeling deep in my stomach. "You aren't a Rabbi. So I don't understand how the synagogue takes up literally every moment of your time. I'm a nurse."

"I know."

"I'm literally on call most of the time, but I still make time for you, I still try to make this work."

"Sara, I'm—"

"Don't you dare fucking say you are sorry!" she snapped at me.

I fell silent, unsure what to say. She was angrier than I had ever seen before, and I couldn't think of a single thing to say that wouldn't set her off more.

"I can't be the only one, Ze'ev. I can't. I need you to care about us as much as I do, I deserve that. I'm a catch, goddamnit."

"You are! I do ... I do, Sara."

"Then why don't you act like it?"

I was dumbstruck. What could I say? Because my life hunting down practitioners of evil magic, ghosts, and werewolves was a priority over her? Because nearly everything she knew about me was a lie? Because at the end of the day, "I don't know, Sara, I try my best."

"Your best is pretty shitty, Zev, and I deserve better."

Her words struck me like a punch to the gut. They weren't said in anger or rage, they were stated softly and sadly. I could feel my relationship crumbling to sand in my hands while I desperately tried to hold it together.

"You do," I finally said. "You do. Please let me make it up to you. Let me be that better; I do love you."

She let out a laugh, the sort of laugh that exists on the verge of a sob or a scream, coming out strangled and unsure what it actually wanted to be.

"Relationships take work, and I need you to put in your share. I need you to not take me for granted."

"I know, I'm sorry."

"I'm so sick of your sorries, your excuses. I don't want you to leave, but you are on thin fucking ice." She whapped her fist against my chest in a half-hearted punch, then sniffled and leaned into me, letting me wrap my arms around her. We stood like that for several minutes in silence, just enjoying the warmth, staving off the fear of an uncertain future for a moment.

"Okay," she finally said, pulling away. "I think I'm too tired to do anything but watch a movie now. But you are spending the night, and you can't complain about Toof's farts."

I smiled, too relieved to even feign irritation or outrage.

"Deal. I love you, Sara."

"Me too," she answered before finding her place on the couch and looking up at me expectantly.

I sat down, and Sara laid on my lap, joined a few moments later by 60 pounds of bulldog that tried to mold into my side. We spent the rest of the night like that, letting Jackie Chan and Jet Li fights lull us to an exhausted slumber.

Chapter 6

My eyes were closed, and the radio was playing. The bus was supposed to have gotten here half an hour ago, but of course, part of the fun of taking the bus is being at the whim of traffic. The morning with Sara had been like a bruise—the pain was visible, still hurt, but if you ignored it and didn't prod at it, you could almost go about living normally. And that's what we did. We didn't mention the fight, didn't mention the anger or my short comings. But they were still there, still screaming in my head, dredging up insecurity and fear. I imagined she felt the same way, angry and hurt but trying her best to be okay. I considered texting her, but I had seen her just before she left for work, and we weren't teenagers, even if she made me feel like one sometimes.

The voice of Steve Earl floated from the speakers to me, good Texas songwriter music. Existing somewhere on the edge of folk rock and bluegrass. Even with my anxiety at an eleven over Sara, the moment was nice. The inside of my car, in the light of day, around other human people, felt like the safest I had been in weeks. And with my eyes shut and music playing, I didn't have to think about anything in particular except how I was supposed to impress a teenage girl. And how my life had come to a place and time where I, a grown ass man, needed to impress a teenage girl.

I heard my phone chime, and I opened an eye to glance down. A text from a Memphis number. I should probably go ahead and program Sandy into my phone ...

We just parked at the station.

It was show time. I don't like being in charge of others. Even if I was Rivkah's boss, I thought of us more as a team, and now we were a team that was responsible for a girl's education. I turned off the car and got out to scan the heads of the people getting off busses. It took several minutes before I saw Sandy. I only barely recognized her. Teenagers grew and changed so much so quickly, and in the last year, she had transitioned from a young bat mitzvah girl to the gangly awkwardness of being a full-fledged teenager. She was all angles and elbows, but looked so typical of a gen Zeenager. I watched her gathering her things from the side of the bus, two massive suitcases and a backpack, enough to get through the semester. I was relieved that she didn't look sad. She looked determined. Determined to take control of her life and the situation. I could definitely respect that. She spotted me quickly. I didn't know if she remembered me from my visit or just assumed the only obviously Jewish guy was there to pick her up, but as soon as she spotted me, she made a beeline in my direction.

Having made contact, I scanned the crowd. Changing cities wouldn't throw the Sheydim off her trail, but at the same time, they were unlikely to show up in the middle of the day in the middle of a crowded Greyhound station. But I could always be wrong.

I was wrong now.

I spotted the cop who had pulled me over by the door of the bus stop. Seeing me looking his way, he tipped his head and tapped his glasses. I didn't take my eyes off him as Sandy made it to my side. She followed my gaze, and I saw her stiffen in my peripheral.

"Why is that cop watching us?" she asked.

"Not a cop—well, not a human cop anyway—and I don't know yet." Not the way I wanted to start off my relationship with this girl—with something scary hunting me and not having any answers. But such was life. I turned my back on the nightmare Sheyd and popped my trunk. "Welcome to Austin, Sandy. I know we've met, but I'm Ze'ev. I'll be teaching you about things like, well, him." I jerked my thumb back toward where the cop was standing. It was a bravado I didn't feel, but I had to put up a front now. Sandy needed to feel confident that I could protect her from the things she was running from.

"Yeah, Rabbi Schulman explained it to me. He said that you were a best at this sort of thing." My eyebrows must have shot up off my head in surprise; receiving a compliment from Nathan was a rare thing. "He also said you were a bad example of Jewish living," she finished. That made more sense.

"Well, Rabbi Schulman is opinionated and ultra-orthodox, whereas I tend to believe that HaShem cares less about the little things and more about kindness." I shrugged and hefted her second bag into the trunk. It felt heavy, but I wasn't about to start off my relationship with this girl by brow-beating her about how many clothes she packed. That was the least of anyone's worries. I would let Rivkah worry about all those logistics. My job was to prepare her for a life that was plagued by the supernatural. Whatever that would look like.

"I'm sorry, are we just ignoring the cop?" The fear cracked her voice, but she still sounded defiant. And tired.

I had to remind myself that she had been faced with being stalked by these things for probably months now. She was tired of running and hiding. She was tired of being prey.

"Yeah, for now. First lesson," I said as I moved around the car and opened the door for her. "We share this world with all manner of creatures. Most of them aren't any more dangerous than other people or a stranger's dog. We leave them alone, they leave us alone." When she got in, I shut her door and got in on my side. "It can be hard to remember, but think of it like this ... those things you're aware of now? They were there before; you just didn't notice them."

She looked skeptical, and I didn't blame her. It was true that the supernatural was always around us. The world was stranger and more wonderful than most people would ever be aware of, but that didn't mean that they had ever been in such close proximity or that they had been watching her before the incident last year. But she had been an unknown to them, a sudden beacon in the gloom of mundane humanity to attract them like moths. Now she was with me, a known player within the realms and circles they traveled in. I hoped that would dissuade the Sheydim, or at the very least decrease their curiosity, redirect them.

"So, what, they're more scared of me than I am of them?"

"No, don't ... don't get it twisted. They aren't scared of us, at all. But they also aren't overly interested in us."

"They seem pretty interested to me."

"Well." She had a point. "That's because you're a new person. They're curious. Are you hungry?"

I wasn't. Just the sight of the unnamed cop had sent my stomach twisting in painful knots, but she didn't need to know that. She looked surprised at the question.

"Yeah, I guess. The rabbi said I would be staying with a girl."

"A woman, yeah. Rivkah, she'll meet us for lunch. We'll give her all of your stuff and then head to the, well, where you're going to be doing most of your studying with me."

She looked relieved to not be staying with me. I didn't blame her. What teenage girl would want to stay with some weird older guy?

"He also said I would still be going to school; he sort of made it sound like all I would be doing is studying and doing homework all the time ..."

That made me roll my eyes a little.

"You have to understand, Sandy, that's Rabbi Schulman's idea of fun. He loves studying." So did I, but she didn't need to hear that. "Yes, you'll be going to school, and yes, we will be studying together and learning a lot; but we'll make sure you have plenty of time to still be a ..." I almost said kid, she would hate that. I remembered my own sister when she was 14. "A young woman," I finished. "You can insta and snap and I'm not going to stop you from going to the mall or date or whatever else you need to do to be happy." I pulled out of the bus stop, glancing over at her as I merged with the idiotic Austin traffic. "Look, none of this is a punishment. This is all meant to give you the tools you need to keep safe, I promise."

✡

The rest of the day went surprisingly smoothly.

While I had been worried that Sandy would be angry and resentful to be staying with us, she had been blown away by Rivkah. It's likely living in Memphis like Sandy had, she hadn't had much exposure to the wide array of Judaism that could be on display outside of the southern United States. I had enjoyed watching her mind racing when I had introduced her to the edgy gothiness that was my assistant—ripped fishnets and all. Rivkah insisted on Ethiopian for lunch, and over lunch, we had explained the logistics of Sandy's new arrangements while she stayed with us.

As promised, Nathan had cut through red tape and gotten Sandy enrolled in the Austin Jewish Academy, a private Jewish school that would be a decent place for her to get an education. Not perfect, in my opinion, but I didn't have all that much say in it. I felt that she would do better to surround herself with a multifaceted sampling of culture and population. Not for any esoteric reason, I simply felt that the pluralist approach to society was a healthier one than being completely insular. It was helpful to understand that sometimes we as Jews didn't have the entire picture that a Jewish Academy might try to paint for her. It would also be a fair amount of culture shock for her since she had attended a secular city school in Memphis. Finally, I wasn't a fan of how far north the school was. While it was nestled in the Dell Jewish Community Center, I was still on the south edge of town, and so was my lab. Rivkah blessedly lived north of town, so it wasn't as brutal for her, though it still wasn't perfect.

By the end of lunch, Sandy had transformed from a weary teen forced into a prison of strangers and constant study to a young girl who was excited to experience the mythical mecca of Austin. Thank HaShem for Rivkah. After lunch, I transferred

Sandy's bags to Rivkah's little VW bug and waved them on their way. Rivkah would spend the week getting to know Sandy and getting her set up at home and in town. I had no doubt they would be planning all sorts of things and made note to remind Rivkah that Sandy was too young to get tattoos or piercings and that maybe we should talk to her parents before we dyed her hair any unnatural colors. Not that I would stop them from having their fun.

After lunch, I killed a few hours at the lab. I had spent so much time pursuing necromancers that I had let my other work go unfinished. Well, not really unfinished, just lapsed. Over the centuries of the Diaspora, Jews had adopted and explored hundreds if not thousands of paths towards magic and spirituality. When I wasn't actively on a "case," I was usually maintaining small hydroponic gardens of rare ingredients to use in alchemy, building a backstock of talismans and amulets, or just researching. And I had a lot of all of that to catch up on. I needed to research werewolves, catch a killer, and I still had that book that Grin had texted me a few nights ago to find. All of that added up to not really having time "to kill".

But I took it anyway. It was rare to be at the lab without Rivkah, and as much as I cherished her help and friendship, her constant "music" could grate against my nerves. We had finally agreed on a joint custody arrangement for the music played in the lab, switching who controlled the music and when. But when she wasn't around, I could work in silence. I enjoyed that silence now. I stood in front of my little garden and trimmed dead leaves. The sound of the clipper blades scraping against one another followed by the near silent fall of dead leaves to the soil underneath was a soothing balm to a tired soul.

I considered the ramifications of pruning a plant, cutting off the diseased and dead parts in order to promote healing and growth. Nowadays, that was common pop psychology, ridding yourself of toxic people in order to be healthier. I wasn't sure I always agreed. Sometimes I felt like through learning to deal with and to stomach those that were unpleasant, we could become better ourselves. Yah knows I wasn't always the best person. I'm not even sure if I'm good now. But I do try my best to be a positive force in the world. A net positive for those around me.

Potions and alchemy isn't a huge part of any path in Judaism, but it was never really outlawed or declared forbidden, other than the use of certain treif ingredients or using potions to contact that dead, things that were covered by other laws. So I had been pretty free to explore the wild world of customs and practices from around the world. Of course, I also had my psilocybin farm, for use in mind expanding meditative practices. Again, not actually forbidden in Jewish practice, just not always smiled upon. The fact that it was being considered for therapeutic uses meant little to me personally, but I felt it was a move in the right direction. Generally speaking, the tinctures and concoctions I created were about changing your state of mind or enhancing natural abilities. They were grosser, more dangerous, and less powerful that uttering the true pronunciation of Hebrew letters, but at the same time, it was less damaging to my body and mind. Like everything, it was a balance between risk and reward.

But all of that aside, gardening in my little private garden was a fantastic way for me to calm my nerves. Or it would have been if my phone hadn't started vibrating on my desk as soon as I got started. I sat there for a minute staring at my phone, clippers in my hand. Exhaustion hit me like a truck. I knew it wasn't because of the phone, but it felt like it. It felt like that buzz had sapped my will to keep going. I remembered the fight I had with Sara, the countless nights I spent casing a house. Kristine's death. That hit me like a physical blow. I had been so busy that I had shut it out.

I ignored my phone for the moment, set down my clippers, and wept.

I'm not proud I cried, but I'm not ashamed; I couldn't even tell you why. Of course, I felt grief over her death, horror at how she had been killed, and sorrow over my own inability to save her. But the truth is I was overwhelmed. I was beaten down by a life that demanded everything of me, on every front, all of the time. In the past, I had always had time to unwind and decompress, pretend at normality for a moment. Or at least what passed for normality for me. I could tend my garden and read books and go home at night and watch whatever dumb cooking show was on streaming to turn off my brain for a moment. Ever since I had gone to Memphis, things had been unrelenting.

My phone buzzed again, insistently. I considered ignoring it. I had ignored all of my social and professional obligations for weeks, what was another bit of time? Maybe that could be my life from now on; I could slip into the darkness and find a cave somewhere far away from the monsters I was tasked to hunt. But even if I did that, the reality of the situation is that the monsters would find me anyway. Wiping my eyes in a futile attempt to rub away the sorrow and frustration that nestled deep in my throat, I walked over to my desk and picked up the phone. One missed call from Alex and one text from Alex. He had the hair sample for me and was on his way. Time to go.

I opened the door and stepped outside … and a

large shadow with a large knife lunged at me.

✡

"Remember me, motherfucker?" The man standing in front of me was pudgy and disheveled. He looked like a middle-aged computer programmer who had been camping out in front of Best Buy for the next console release for a couple of days. Though the large knife he was waving in my face did a bit to dispel the pathetic vibe, it only heightened the manic desperation that fell off of him in waves.

"Attback, I assume." I raised my hands in a show of surrender. Even though we had never actually met, I had studied his picture and his life fairly closely before breaking into his house and training the cops on him. The long strip of scarlet silk tied to his knife fluttered in the breeze, and I wondered where he had been hiding that. Why was this bit of cloth important enough to keep clean when he himself reeked of BO and stale sweat? He must have been on the run and essentially living on whatever cash he had on hand when he had left the house a few nights ago. How he had found me, specifically found my lab, was worrisome.

"I don't think we've had the pleasure, actually."

"Fuck you, you fuck, you stupid Jewish fuck. Because of you, everyone thinks I'm a Satanist. Because of you, I've lost everything. The Order, my home, my job … I had a family, damnit."

"And that's my fault?"

"I know it was you. I know it was you who called the cops and came into our house." He was snarling at me, the tip of his ridiculous looking knife shaking in front of me. "I know it was you that ruined everything."

"I'm pretty sure I didn't convince you to join an

insane cult and murder people, actually, I think that one's all on you." I wasn't worried; I wasn't scared in the least. The last time one of the cultists came at me with a knife, he had been on drugs and refreshed. Attback might have been dangerous if he hadn't wanted to yell at me first. But as tired as I was, his own exhaustion was wearing on him more.

"I'm going to take everything from you. I'm going to kill your family and friends. I'm going to raise them from the dead and force them to eat you alive while their souls watch. I want you to understand that; I want you to see it co—"

I'm sure what he was about to say was *coming,* but it was hard for him to speak with a mouth full of broken teeth and blood. I had reached the end of my patience so had stepped inside his reach and delivered a punch right to his sweaty face.

He stumbled back, clutching at his ruined mouth. I stepped back and pulled out my Jericho, a handgun I had gotten used to during my time in the IDF, and leveled it at his head.

"I would drop the knife, Alan." Part of me wanted to blow his brains out, to murder him in cold blood the way he had killed others, the way he'd had Kristine killed. The Jericho was a large enough caliber that it could leave very little of his face intact for an open casket funeral. The same thing he had denied Kristine. My rage begged me to pull the trigger. It urged me to end him and be done with him.

It looked like he was considering taking a run at me even with my gun leveled at him, but then he smiled, that wide crazy-ass smile of a person who feels they've won. It wasn't much of a warning, but it was enough for me to brace for the impact as Ansar Mullhani charged out of the bushes nearby and tackled me. He carried me to the ground, smelling just as fresh as Attback looked. I wasn't sure what his plan had been, but apparently, it didn't involve me keeping my grip on the hand gun or punching him in the kidney repeatedly. He howled in pain and used both hands to try to restrain my gun hand. I could see Attback getting to his feet and going to grab his knife.

I stopped punching and gripped Mullhani's face. "V'mareh kebod Adonai ke'es okelet!" I meant to whisper the words, but they came out as a guttural roar. The flame erupted from my hand and engulfed his head. My rage was powering my intention. I had been mourning their victims, and then they showed up eager for their justice. The flames gutted out as soon as they appeared, my own surprise at them breaking my concentration. But it was enough. He scrambled back from me, screaming in pain and fear. He would live with those burns the rest of his life.

As I regained my feet, I considered what that would mean, what amount of life did he have left? I could shoot them both now, I could put both of them in the ground. I raised the gun. Attback was begging, begging for his life after he had just threatened to have my friends and family eat me as living dead. Mullhani was a whimpering sack unable to think past the pain. I didn't lower the gun, I just held Attback in my sights, my own smile growing wider and wider as Alex Barman drove up to find two of America's most wanted serial killers held at gunpoint.

Chapter 7

What should have been a quiet night was turning into a circus. Alex couldn't just shove the two of them in his car and call it a night. These two were too big of a deal. And so there I was, hours later, sitting on the steps of a warehouse as police swarmed the area. There was some question as to whether Mullhani would need to go to the hospital for his burns, but I think they were mostly curious about what had caused them. Alex came and sat heavily next to me.

"Why are you always in the middle of the weirdest fucking cases, Ze'ev?" he asked me.

I had to laugh at that. I would love to tell him, but what could I say?

"Just lucky, I guess. I think they probably blame me for their little fan club falling apart." I had gotten through this scuffle without so much as a scrape or a black eye. No stitches needed, thank HaShem.

"Why now, is my question. I mean, why come after you while they're on the run and known?" Alex shook his head at my nonchalance.

It was a good question. I knew the answer, of course; they came after me because I had exposed them. I was the reason they had been on the run. "Their sense of vengeance outweighed their sense of self-preservation."

Alex considered that for a moment and shrugged. "They claim that you caused the burns on Mullhani."

"How would I have done that?"

"I don't know, man, do you have a ..." Alex trailed off, unsure of what he was even asking.

"A flamethrower? Were you going to ask me if I have a flamethrower? Why would I have a personal flamethrower? How should I know what an insane person thinks?" Two questions in one answer; I was on a roll. I was feeling a mix of elation and frustration. On one hand, I hadn't gotten to take my anger out on the cultists. Maybe that was HaShem saving me from my own rage by taking the opportunity for violence away. On the other hand, I was happy these two would be off the street and in prison. Though I had to hope they wouldn't be in the same cell block as Basken. That's all I needed, a prison necromancer cult.

"Yeah, sorry," Alex finally said, unable to think of a way to get around the ridiculousness of the accusation. The two killers were screaming about magic and a magical war that was coming to sweep away the human debris that cluttered the world. They were unquestionably insane. "You're kind of a badass, Ze'ev."

"Why should I be a badass? I'm just trying to survive. People like this make it more difficult." I gestured at the squad car where the two men were cuffed and ranting. "Do you have the hair sample?"

Alex nodded and pulled a small bag from his pocket. He gave a quick look around before handing it to me.

"Holy shit, man." I laughed. "You would make a terrible drug dealer. Stop looking so furtive. This helps, thank you."

"How does it help? I mean, what can you tell about it that we couldn't?"

The closer I got with people, the more I worked with them, the harder it was to hide things from them. It made it a little lonely at times. But I would sound just as insane as the cultists if I told him the truth.

"I have contacts that can do a bit of a deep dive, may help me narrow down where this killer is." I leaned back against the steps, resting my elbows behind me. I needed to let Sara know what happened. She would be seeing it on the news, and last time I didn't tell her that one of these guys had attacked me, she had been pretty angry. "Look, the sooner I get clear of this mess, the sooner I can work on these samples."

Alex nodded and stood, looking down at me. "Okay, I'll see if I can't expedite this at all, but expect us to need you to come down to the station for paperwork and questions. This is the second time you've been in the middle of this mess; people will be curious."

"When are they not?" I asked, waving at him.

True to his word, he had rounded up the police and gotten everyone off within a few minutes. I was free to do a bit of sleuthing myself now.

✡

I headed back into the warehouse lab. There was a temptation to go back to the garden, my little corner of Zen, but I was amped up now. Adrenaline had been pumped through my system, and I doubted I could sit still. Luckily, I had another path forward with my night. I pulled a map of the Austin area out of a drawer and moved to the far wall to tape the map up. I smoothed it out with my hands, my fingers lingering over the lines of the roads. This wasn't a completely up to date map, but it was hard to have an accurate up to date map of a city that was constantly growing and changing. Austin had gone from the live music capital of the world to the construction capital. A definite downgrade.

The Torah forbids certain acts of divination. The Talmud goes further to ban the practice entirely. But that hadn't stopped Jewish mystics throughout the ages from experimenting with different forms of divination. I had my own theories on why it had been banned. First and foremost, a lot of divination relied on spirits and necromancy, and any communication with the dead was forbidden. Secondly, and this was a stretch, I think that prophecy was a commodity, something to be protected and kept only to elites. If anyone could experience prophecy, then what was special about it? What I was doing now, though technically a form of divination, didn't touch either of those issues.

Belomancy, divination using arrows, could be used in a lot of different ways. You could use special arrows, jumble them in a quiver and see which one you pulled, or cast them like runes. You could shoot a bunch of them into the sky and see where they landed and try to divine prophecy from that. But my method would be a lot simpler and a lot cleaner. I used a bit of tape to secure a couple of the hairs from the baggy Alex had given me to an arrow and then sat before the map to meditate while holding the arrow. I cleared my head as best I could, concentrating on the idea of finding where this hair came from. Concentrating on finding and punishing this monster. I was fueled by the fact that a second child had gone missing. I wrapped my attention around the arrow, my fingers tracing over the wood grain of the shaft and the tufts of feathers in the fletching. I didn't make this arrow—I didn't make the arrow myself, I didn't have the expertise—but it had been handmade—almost anything involved in magic needed to be handmade—using older techniques. The painstaking nature of the work infused the objects with the intention, with the energy of its creation.

I sat there, quiet for the most part, though I did hum a niggun to myself—a sort of wordless mantra to focus my mind even further. I pictured the Lekowitz child, the missing girl. I pictured Alex's little girl. I focused on them. I brought them into my mindfulness, pushing the need to find one and avenge the other into every fiber of the arrow in my hands. When I couldn't anymore, when my own sorrow threatened to overcome my senses, I stood and retrieved the small bow I kept in the closet next to the arrows. The bow was nothing special, just a normal hunting bow bought at a big box store while it was on sale. The bow wasn't the important part of this ritual. I pulled the bowstring back and took aim at the map of Austin on the wall opposite of where I stood. Just enough of an aim to ensure I wasn't shooting in the wrong direction. I closed my eyes and let the arrow loose.

I could feel the pull on my energy, on my *self*, as the arrow flew away from me and thunked into the wall. I let go of a deep breath I had been holding and opened my eyes. The arrow jutted from the wall on the southeastern edge of the map, the Bastrop area. That made some sense. If there were any big wild animals, especially something that could pass for a wolf or a coyote, they would be out there amongst the pine trees. It was late now, I could wait until morning. I wasn't on a schedule, no one would yell at me for not hustling. Except I was on a timetable. Whatever had taken Hayley and killed her now had another kid. Maybe she would be okay if I went home and crawled in bed. But maybe she wouldn't. The image of Kristine flashed in my mind. Could I have saved her if I had spent less time casing the house? A growl bubbled up from deep in my chest. I took note of where the arrow had punctured the map, pulled it out of the wall, and headed out.

Chapter 8

I always thought that Bastrop smelled like burning. It didn't, not anymore. Twice it had burned, arson was likely, but unlike some other parts of the country, big forest fires and wild fires were a big deal here in Texas, it wasn't something we were used to. It had taken years for any of the pine woods of Bastrop to grow back, and it still wasn't entirely healed. The burnt skeletons of trees reached up into the warm Texas night, grasping for something that they would never reach. The morbid part of my mind pictured them not as limbs and branches but the skeletal remains of children's arms grasping for help. I shook that image out of my head quickly, driving alone on a dark Texas back road, one hand on the wheel while the other gripped the arrow tightly. The trees weren't scary, but the things between them could be. I imagined I could see the pin pricks light reflected off of predatory eyes between the trees on either side of road.

I hadn't been bothered by the ghouls since Grin had arrived in my apartment months ago. They either assumed I was dead or had been ordered to leave me alone. I hoped it was the latter; the last thing I needed added to the mix was more monsters hungry for blood. The thought of Grin made me think of the eyeless cop that had been stalking me lately. If he was following me, I was presenting him with an excellent opportunity to get me alone. I thought of maybe escaping this life of hunting down monsters for a calmer existence of maybe teaching, hell maybe even teaching for the Beit Din. It was a pipe dream. So long as I was mobile, Nathan would have me chasing beasts; and if I did ever get to the point where my body was too broken to continue, he would just put some other poor sucker in my place.

I could feel the arrow tugging gently in my grasp, guiding me towards something. I was hopeful it would lead me to a still living child. That was my biggest dream, that I could rescue a kid and then call in the police to deal with whatever evidence was there, and I wouldn't have to hunt down a monster in the backwoods of the Texas wilderness. I pulled over on the side of the road when the arrow tugged towards the tree line. I would need to leave my car here and venture into the woods to follow the guidance of the arrow. And out there, I would be fair game for whatever was in the woods, natural or not.

The mental image of ghouls reaching out to snatch me or of large slavering wolf-men emerging from shadows made my stomach drop. But again, if I did nothing, I would never be able to forgive myself. I needed to make tougher friends. I couldn't drag Rivkah out here, I needed some badass who enjoyed shooting and hunting and making a mess of things. Of course, my Rolodex for hunting supernatural creatures was pretty small. There were a few others I had met over the years. Mostly holy men of other traditions, priests and preachers, monks and imams. They each had their own methods, their own tasks. But generally speaking, we got along just fine. The truth was most holy men I had met were more concerned with making sure they got to the donation tray than protecting the community, and those that did protect did so from the shadows, like I did.

I was far enough off the highway and main roads of Bastrop that I felt it should be safe leaving my car unattended here, though I suppose safe was a relative term. I retrieved my Jericho from its home under the driver's seat and slipped it into the shoulder holster under my jacket. I hoofed it through the woods, away from my car. Luckily, the moon was high in the sky now; it wasn't too difficult to see, and I wanted to avoid using my flashlight or phone for light. There were certain spells and prayers that could be used to enhance my night vision or light my way. But after barbecuing Mullhani's head, I was a little hesitant to tap into the supernal powers. I was running too hot. I assumed that's what was going on, it wasn't like I could turn to a group of peer reviewed researchers on magical theory. Something that Rivkah hoped to change. I hoped so too. I know that magic, and Jewish magic in particular, would never be accepted as a mainstream science, but it would be nice to be less alone.

I passed through the trees as quietly as I could. I was a special services trained soldier, but all of my combat experience and know-how was for inner city fighting, and I had never been trained for fighting or tracking in the forests—probably because there wasn't a whole lot of forest to be had in Israel. I paused next to a tree, closing my eyes for a moment and letting my eyes adjust to the darkness a bit more before letting the arrow rest lightly in my palm. It twitched, slowly aligning itself with, well, I didn't know what it was aligning with yet. But that's where I would head. I glanced at my smart-watch, an anniversary gift from Sara, which she had hoped would make me better at keeping track of appointments. It hadn't. Lucky for me, it had a GPS and compass built in. I was a bit worried; while I knew I was in the general right area because of the map, the arrow was now only showing me basic direction. It could be miles away, or I could stumble on a werewolf when I stepped past the next tree. I had no way of knowing.

Every faith has to ask the questions about the existence of evil. Sometimes we try to ignore it, but it's always there. If you believe in God, you have to try to figure out why anything worth worshiping would allow evil to exist. In dual religions where there were evil deities, that was easy. The devil exists, so we can just chalk it up to that. In religions with no devil, with no evil being at the bottom of every plot of inconvenience, you had a real problem. Rabbi had argued and thought and pondered this question for as long as there had been rabbi. I couldn't claim to be smarter than them. As I climbed over a large exposed root, I considered the question myself, something to keep my mind off of the insanity of my actions or the way the shadows of the trees around me swayed like grasping claws with every breeze.

The problem was twofold, in my opinion. On one hand, you had human evil, acts of greed and violence. Lawmakers damning their country to a slow death by pollution for a few more dollars to line their pockets, rapists, murderers, the whole pantheon of deadly sins enacted by human beings. Again, it was an easy solution: "free will". So long as people had free will, we could excuse HaShem for any evil deed because it was not the blessed holy one, it was a person. On the other hand, there were acts of nature, hurricanes, typhoons, children born with horrible birth defects. The kinds of things where no one was to blame. These were the hardest to countenance. What kind of merciful god would wipe out thousands in a natural disaster?

It was easy to just say these are the rules of nature, a way for the world to exist, that we must accept the bad with the good. But that was lazy. Why would we need to accept the bad in light of a truly omnipotent deity? Fundamentalists would claim that when we were tossed from the Garden of Eden, we were tossed from a perfect world with no misfortune. That it was our sin of eating an apple that had caused all of this woe. Again, lazy, lazy and boring. My entire faith had built itself on seeking answers, arguing and studying and learning as much as we could. Study was as close to a holy ritual as any actual rituals in Judaism, so I refused to believe that seeking knowledge is what condemned us all to the existence of evil.

Some people thought that during the big bang, during the creation, that the light of the divine shattered and evil was the cracks in creation, and through loving kindness, you could seal those cracks. I liked this analogy; after all, the idea was that the better we made the world for people, the less likely they would be to bring pain into it. A nice thought, but I doubted giving food to the homeless would stop any earthquakes or tornadoes. Others tried to explain that while HaShem had created the world and had brought order to it, the natural state of all things was chaos and entropy. Evil, both deeds and natural disasters that struck tragedy against our combined human experience, was creation trying to buck the order and return to its natural state of chaos. I didn't really buy this either, it was too nihilist, too bleak. But at the same time, I had to admit that it had a certain appeal to it.

Perhaps it was this return to chaos that had inspired my thoughts away from what I was doing, pulling me from mindfulness to being oblivious to my surroundings. My foot caught a root, and I tumbled forward hard, rolling as I hit the ground into a clearing that led to a small shack in the middle of the woods. I dropped the arrow somewhere in the roots. Everything was dark, but from beyond the shed, I could see a light, the main house, probably.

It was surreal to find this ramshackle home in the middle of the remains of the Bastrop woods. It would have surely been consumed by the fires when they swept through. But there was a clear line where the remnants of burnt trees and grass stopped. I walked forward slowly. I was looking for a killer, a monster, and I was in Texas. Even if this property didn't belong to a killer, they would probably have a gun specifically for people trespassing on their property.

Creeping forward felt wrong. I was trespassing, but a child's life was in danger. I would risk it. I paused at the very edge, where the regrowth of a forest that had been through a conflagration met with the dry, dead, and untouched soil. I could feel the tingle of magic. Tingle may be the wrong word, but when you do or are around enough magic, it leaves a feeling in the air, like the atmosphere just after the rain comes, like ozone charging towards a lightning strike. I walked around the line between the world inside the protective spells that kept this shack standing up and the world outside. Understanding what traditions of magic caused this could go a long way to understanding what I was dealing with.

After a few steps, I found what I was looking for: a simple stake of wood with a cow skull lashed to it with barbed wire. Something like this wouldn't be too out of place anywhere in Texas, really, especially not next to the house of some deep-woods jackass. But in the wood, I could see old symbols carved, Norse runes, Greek letters, and more, a hodgepodge of symbols that spoke to a melting pot of traditions. Not common to any but those who carried the most ancient paths of 'Granny Magic'. I used my camera to take a picture of the totem, hoping the flash wouldn't draw attention. This wasn't a smoking gun, not really, plenty of Appalachian wise women put these sorts of things to ward off disaster or, more likely, the law from poking around their still. I had a friend who could tell me more when I was back home.

A lot of people demonized the backwaters folk and the uneducated. While they tended to have some pretty ass-backwards ideas, they also generally weren't bad people. I needed more evidence of foul play before I called in the cops on some poor hick using magic to hide from the government. I looked through the window on the little shack. It was darker inside than outside. I grabbed my phone again and opened the flashlight app so I could see through the window and fell back with a curse as a large face appeared in the darkness of the shack, smiling and wild eyed. I turned to run and was confronted by a massive wolf.

There aren't many wolves in Texas, those that are here are both endangered and closer to coyotes in size than the wolves popularized in the media. This was not the sort of wolf you found in Texas. To find a wolf like this, you would need to go the Rockies, or more likely Canada. It was huge, easily 150 pounds of muscle and probably close to seven feet long. Its teeth were bared in warning, and I didn't dare move. I heard the door of the shack open and close behind me. Footsteps crunched through the dead leaves as the man approached.

"Well, well, well! Lookey what decided to come on to my property here." The voice rumbled out, but instead of possessing that Texas twang accent that I knew and loved, his accent sounded more Nordic, like he had come from Sweden or Poland originally. I didn't dare turn my back on the wolf. I had no idea how it would react, but I knew most predators tended to really get worked up when prey ran from them. The man behind me let out a chuckle that was low and dangerous, reminding me of the full-throated growl that was brewing in the wolf. I was surprised I hadn't heard the sound of a shotgun being racked yet, but the man must have assumed the wolf would be enough of a deterrent.

"I'm sorry, I was looking for a phone. I'm not trying to—"

"Ya know what I hate, Betsie?"

The wolf, presumably Betsie, cocked her head and padded past me. I turned as she passed, keeping her in my line of sight. She sat down on her haunches next to a massive man, a veritable Goliath. The mountain of muscle, presumably a man, in front of me was dressed in denim overalls and a plaid shirt. His arms, as thick as my thighs, were hairy. The man looked like Michael Clarke Duncan—if Michael Clarke Duncan had been pasty white—and sported a massive bushy beard. His teeth glinted behind the red curls of his beard as he looked me up and down. "I hate a liar."

"No, no lies. I parked over off of the road and was walking to clear my head." I slowly tried to stand up straight, making myself as big as I could next to the massive man. "Fighting with my girlfriend." Most successful lies had nuggets of truth; I could only hope he would believe mine. "I got lost while walking and was hoping to find someone that could help me get back to the road."

He lifted his head and sniffed at the air, exaggerated motions as though he were making a show of it. The wolf mimicked the motion. I got the impression he was mocking me.

"Yeah? Well, that's too bad, buddy, I suppose you always use tracking spells when your ruminating on your woman?"

I was a taken aback. It was rare that anyone outside my immediate circle just brazenly and openly acknowledged magic in any way. Generally speaking, it was only colleagues, of which there were few, and people like Basken who wanted me dead. I only had a few choices here: I could continue to lie and hope I could bluff my way out of whatever fate this backwoods giant had in mind for me or I could attempt at honesty.

"You can smell that? Or did I trip your ward back there?" I asked, jerking my thumb back to the cow skull totem.

"I don't much feel like answering questions. Why are you out here?" The huge man crossed his arms over his chest.

"I'm looking for someone."

From where they were, I felt like I could probably draw on them before they could get to me; it gave me some confidence. Maybe it wasn't a werewolf, maybe this monster was just a human that shared his victims with his pet. We stood in silence for a moment. I pressed outward with my senses, seeking any sounds or signs that I could use to my advantage. But no matter how much I had trained myself to be aware, I wasn't going to outdo an actual wolf. I let my hands hover, palm down near my chest, a universal sign for 'let's all keep calm'.

"Well, you found me," the man said after several long minutes. His tone was assured, as though he were deescalating the tension, but his body remained tense, the wolf at his side remained coiled to spring. It seemed we were both attempting to lure the other into a false sense of security. There was no question in my mind now; this was the killer, this was the abductor. If I could survive this meeting, I could call the police and give them directions. Even a big ass giant and his wolf couldn't throw off a swat team. I hoped.

"Yep. You. I found you." I don't know if it was doubt that kept me from drawing first or fear. But no matter the reason, the wolf was at my throat before I could reach for my gun. Her teeth closed down on my arm, my jacket shielding me from the worst of it, but only barely. These jaws would crush my bones if I allowed them to. I kicked out with my legs as she carried me down. I could hear the ginger hick laughing as I struggled. Is this how he killed the children? By letting his wolf tear them apart? I wouldn't die that way. I pulled the wolf's head close, wrapping my arm around it, and jammed my finger into its eye. No magic needed. With a terrified whimper, the wolf dropped my arm and scampered back. It probably only bought me a moment, so I rose and pulled out my Jericho.

The giant was almost on me already.

No time to think.

I fired.

He stopped, looking down at the blood spreading across his chest, and then looked up at me smiling wide, revealing long, sharp, blood flecked teeth. I fired again, hitting him in the chest. He took a step back, not bothering to even look down at the second ragged hole in his body. I raised the gun and fired a third time. His head snapped back, but there was no spray of blood across the clearing, and he didn't fall. He turned his head back to me, revealing the ghastly entry wound that was his left eye, and smiled again. It was my turn to let out a terrified whimper and run.

✡

I fled through the forest as quickly as my legs would carry me, keeping my Jericho in hand. I figured if I had to; I could shoot the wolf, even if the man had proven to be all but immune to bullets. I hadn't expected that. I wasn't thinking clearly anymore, though, I was just fleeing. I had faced down ghouls and zombies and dybbukim, but I had never seen something that took a bullet to the brain and just kept smiling. Tearing through the brush and branches, I could hear the howl of the wolf behind me. They were gaining. I would do everything I could to survive. I forced my fear deep inside me. I had to think clearly if I was going to survive the night. I shoved my gun into the holster as I ran, wishing now that I had brought some heavier firepower or something that amounted to a magical weapon.

I grabbed the butterfly knife I always kept with me, flipped it open, and ducked behind a tree. I prayed I would have enough time as I began carving letters into the bark. Ever since my run in with cults and ghouls, I had been doing more studying of defensive and offensive incantations. Before recently, I only really needed spells and glyphs that would assist in exorcisms. As I carved the strange symbols, copied from books like Ha'Sefer Yeyzirah and the Sefer Ha'Razim, I chanted quickly under my breath the simple phrase 'Atah gabor L'olam Adonai'. Within the seconds, the wind began to pick up, blowing my scent away from the wolf, and a few moments later, it began raining, big fat heavy drops that landed with as much sound as footfalls on the dried leaves of the forest.

With the wind at my back and the rain masking

my sounds, I started running again. I had to be more careful now. I needed to maintain a bit of intention on the magic I had carved into the bark, and I don't have the most amazing sense of direction there is, but I did know I only really needed to flee in the direction I had come from — the benefit of the arrow was it drew in a straight line. So long as I hadn't gotten turned around in the forest, I would make it back to my car. I heard more howls echoing through the forest. I wasn't a biologist; I couldn't discern what kind of wolf or coyote was crashing through the dead branches of the Bastrop forest just by the sound of the baying. But truth be told, I wasn't all that interested in finding out.

I paused and turned, pressing my back to a tree, my fingers closing around a talisman in my pocket. My thumb ran over the groove of the Hebrew letters carved there. I chanted an invocation as I pulled the talisman from my pocket and held it in front of me. We don't pray to angels in Judaism; we don't pray to saints or figure heads, not to the patriarchs or matriarchs. But within the mystic tradition, we do invoke their names. Sometimes as a curse or a method of asking G-d to look after us on behalf of someone better than us. But this was not supplication, this was a demand. I commanded Nuriel, angel of storms, to drive back the attackers. I pushed my intention through the amulet that was carved in Hebrew and older script.

The wind picked up. Lightning struck nearby. I was no longer alone against the literal wolves at the proverbial gates.

I pressed on as the rain continued to grow in strength. Maybe I had overdone it. But I wanted to escape, I also needed to figure out a way to get the police out here quickly. That was easier said than done. The cultist had been in a house in a neighborhood where it was believable that someone could have overheard or seen something illegal happening. Out here in the boonies, it would take a bit more work. I almost wished that those idiots hadn't ambushed me and got themselves arrested; I would have been able to claim I saw them fleeing into the woods.

I almost stumbled as the idea hit me like one of the bolts of lightning cracking overhead. That was it. That was perfect. I pressed on harder now. I had a plan. After what felt like an hour of running, I broke through the tree line and nearly ate it again onto the pavement of the street. I had made it out.

I turned and pulled out my gun, waiting several seconds for the wounded giant or his wolf to emerge from the forest. Water dripped down my face and obscured the already dense shadows of the forest. I was panting, I was dead on my feet. I saw headlights so hid my gun again and turned towards my car, which sat a few dozen feet away. I was sure I wasn't safe now. But I was in a place that I could do what needed to be done.

Chapter 9

My lab was quiet. I sat at my desk, the small TV playing on local news. It had been 30 minutes since I had called the Bastrop County Sheriff's Department screaming about men with knives and robes. Normally that sort of Satanic Panic bullshit wouldn't fly. But with the whole nation currently freaking out over Basken and the two serial killers in Round Rock, everyone was on edge. And considering they had just attacked little old me earlier this evening, a little theatrics would set off a media swarm. Already the news was covering what was about to be a manhunt through the woods. They were also already stretching the little information I had given the sheriff's office into a massive yarn of a second ritual. It was insane, but it was useful.

I glanced down at my phone. It was silent so far, but I assumed any moment now Sara, Rivkah, or Alex would be blowing up my phone. It was just a question of who came for their pound of flesh first. At least Rivkah I could deal with like an informed equal. I didn't have any good lies to tell Sara this time. I would tell her what I had told Alex, that they had attacked me because I had been involved in the take down of Basken; that should work.

I jumped when the teapot I had set on the little heating plate we kept in the lab started whistling. I was too jumpy. I moved over to the little makeshift kitchenette we had put together and poured the hot water over the coffee filter in its little plastic holder that sat on a mug. I watched it drain out and poured a second time before setting the kettle down.

I tossed the grounds in the trash and dug through the mini fridge for creamer. I had to be careful. If I was careless, I would end up drinking one of Rivkah's healthy bullshit milk substitutes. It was bad enough that Sara was always trying to get me to eat healthier or give up certain foods and habits, but I had to deal with Rivkah's health ambushes when she switched out my foods. It wasn't like I was overweight or unhealthy either. I worked out regularly, I maintained an active life style. Hell, I had just outrun a damn werewolf. I poured extra creamer in, just in defiance, before moving back to my table to continue watching the developments. Was I getting too used to sleepless nights filled with danger? It was possible. My mind was becoming wired for constant alertness in a way it hadn't been since I had been in the IDF.

I needed to get a couch for the lab, with as often as one of us ended up pulling an all-nighter here. I would love to curl up on the couch and get comfortable while waiting for something to happen. I set my head on the desk and watched the TV sideways. I wondered how long it would take them to get a chopper in the air, how long it would take them to get the dogs out. I also had to wonder how many cops would die trying to bring the creature down. Would they even be able to? What would happen when an immortal killer was confronted by the police? My stomach churned at the thought that I could be responsible for a death today. I closed my eyes against the wave of nausea.

✡

Jolting awake at the sound of the door opening, I spilled cold coffee across my desk. I cursed under my breath as I tried to rescue papers and books that had been in the path of the cup. I had passed out in my own damn drool before I had even gotten to take a sip. Of course, it was just Rivkah. She bounced in, her usually bubbly and perky self, freshly showered, made up, and ready to face the day. She was wearing a sun dress with a cardigan over her shoulders. She had once told me, after I had teased her about the amount of them she had, that the cardigan was the curvy lady's secret weapon for making outfits work-appropriate. I stopped teasing after that.

"Zev? You're here? Are you okay?" She was surprised.

I was surprised too.

"Yeah, I was watching the news and must have ..." I glanced around my desk, making sure I had gotten all the books and papers off it before I rose to find a towel to clean up the mess. "Must have fallen asleep." I woke the TV up with the remote and watched for a moment, towel in hand. They had found the shack and house in the middle of the woods. It was empty. The goddamn yokel must have run after I left. I sat down heavily, staring at the TV, waiting for any news to be shown. The camera panned around as a Jennifer Sanders explained the situation for what was probably the 100th time. The woman looked exhausted, and I could see why. So was I.

"After I dropped Sandy off at school, I went by your apartment to check on you. I got your messages when I woke up. I can't believe they attacked you here." She was still talking, setting herself up to the day, but I was paying attention to the news.

Behind Ms. Sanders on the TV were empty graves. They weren't the clean holes of the police excavators either, these had been dug up by whoever had run. Sanders was saying something about search dogs being used to comb the area, but so far, they had found seven holes in total. Seven holes. Was that seven corpses? He had left Hayley's body practically on their damn doorstep; if he was burying the dead on his land, why risk capture or discovery by bringing Hayley back? Seven. I wandered over to one of the several bookshelves and pulled a couple of books, flipping through the pages, looking for some sort of meaningful connection to seven corpses buried in the yard.

I was thinking about the possibilities. Maybe he had needed corpses for some sort of ritual but got a taste for murder. Maybe now he couldn't stop himself. Maybe the corpses were like the amulets I carried, and the damage I had done to him had been distributed to rotting corpses in the ground. Maybe he needed more now. Hell, they weren't corpses. My mind shot to someone who would bury living children and use them to protect himself from damage. All of this was mindless speculation. My eyes darted to the safe in the corner of the lab.

Books on treif magic and black rituals. Necromancy, blood magic, vile sorcery, and theory on the summoning and control of demonic entities. The shit that I had been gathering at Grin's demands. The answer to what sort of ritual would require the bodies of seven children was probably in there. My stomach turned just thinking about it. The problem, beyond just the simple forbidden nature of those books, was that they were corrupting. People always assumed that power was corrupting, that you got the power and then you went mad. But the truth, I think, is that you make tiny concessions for power along the way, you do something wrong and get just enough power to do something that's better than the wrong. And it goes like that, with tiny concessions, until suddenly, you're staring down at the masses wondering why you don't just take control of it all.

Hell, if I had spoken to Basken more than cutting his damn hand off, maybe I would have found he had the same story, that he thought I was the villain and he was the hero. Then again, necromancers were fucking edgelords.

"What did you do last night?" Rivkah suddenly asked, making me jump.

I had been so deep in thought I had forgotten she was there.

"Huh?" I asked, caught off guard, feeling like a kid who had been found with his hand in the cookie jar.

Rivkah pointed at the map on the wall and the bow that was out. "Belomancy?" she asked before stalking to the bow and picking it up, gesturing at the TV with it. "And I'm guessing your cop friend showed up with the hair sample?"

I met her angry gaze. I knew what she was going to say before she said it. "Yes, I know, I know you don't like it when I put myself in danger."

"That's beyond dangerous, Ze'ev! I thought we had this talk back in August. Man, you can't just ... you just won't listen." She tossed the bow down and rubbed her eyes, smearing mascara in the process. "Stop acting like a stupid lone wolf. It's shitty, it's toxic, and it's going to get you killed real fast."

I don't know that I agreed with her about my life expectancy. After all, I had made it this far. Besides

... "I don't like putting other people in the line of danger, Rivkah."

"So what did you do? Did you actually traipse out into the middle of the fucking woods by yourself? Did you just walk up to a house in the middle of the woods, where you know a psychopath child murderer is living?" She made it sound so much more dangerous than I had hoped.

"Yes," I finally admitted.

"The storm?" she asked. She didn't need to clarify; the storm I had brought through invoking Nuriel had been too sudden to be natural.

"Yes," I admitted again. I watched her roll her eyes and storm over to her desk to sit in a huff. I sat in silence for a minute before rising to make myself a new cup of coffee. I made Rivkah a cup too.

"Remember how with Basken you were completely fucked until you started asking for help?" she asked suddenly, breaking the tense silence.

"Yeah, Rivkah, I remember."

"And you remember how I sat here and helped you with finding the cultists?"

"Yeah, Rivkah, I remember," I said again. A bad habit I had during arguments was going on autopilot.

"So why did you think this would be better to do on your own? I mean, holy shit, you got attacked here and then thought to yourself *Oh, you know what? Being in mortal danger once isn't enough, I should go confront a LITERAL FUCKING MONSTER in the FUCKING woods!*" She shouted the last part at me. Glaring at the mug of coffee I offered her, she looked like she wanted to slap it out of my hands. After a few moments, she took the cup and turned her back to me, drinking it at her desk, still fuming.

"Rivkah, the truth is, I didn't want to wait. There's

a kid out there, a kid that may still be alive. A kid that is closer to death every goddamn minute I sit around with my thumb up my ass trying to figure this thing out." I stared at her hunched shoulders. It took me a second to realize she was crying. I sat in mute silence unsure how to respond to tears. I moved to her and rested my hand on her back. "Rivkah?"

She looked up at me, her makeup all smudged behind puffy eyes. Somehow, she even made the messy makeup look pretty. She sniffed. "I know, I know. Okay? I know that we're on this time crunch and that we have to do something or else ... what if we're too late?" she finally asked.

I shrugged a little; part of me suspected we were already too late. And who knew where the man had gone after my confrontation yesterday? "I don't know, Rivkah. I don't want to find out. But I'm scared of being too late too." I squeezed her shoulder. I hated seeing her crying. But now at least I understood where her anger was coming from. Fear. I understood fear. It's something I dealt with on a near constant basis.

Fear of monsters, fear of people, fear of disappointment, fear of being called out for the lies I told Sara. Fear of being a failure. I squeezed her shoulder again and started walking to the map of Austin that I had shot arrows at. Where would the man go, now that he had been scared out of his hidey-hole? If he were smart, he would leave the Bastrop area, too much heat there now. It occurred to me that maybe he had also been the arsonist that had done so much damage to the area. Maybe those fires had been used to cover up other crimes. I stood staring at the map, willing it to give me answers.

There was a sudden knock on the door, making both Rivkah and I jump in surprise. We don't get visitors here, and for good reason, this place was set up as a lab for magical knowledge and practices. I moved to the door and glanced at Rivkah. She had reached into her desk for the little hand gun she had started packing after our first run in with the cult and since being on the ghouls' shit list. I opened the door a smidge.

Alex Barman pushed his way past me. I was so surprised that I stepped back, letting him in. Alex was clearly agitated. He glanced at the TV, saw we were watching the news, and looked at me with red rimmed eyes. I wondered when he had last slept.

"Alex—" I began, but he cut me off.

"They think this is the guy who took Hayley." He lifted his hands to his face and rubbed his eyes, trying to rub the exhaustion out of his brain. When he reopened them, he walked further into the workshop and paused, as if noticing all the weird shit for the first time. Rivkah's scientific equipment, the small foundry, the arts, the books, the magic formulae on the white board. The bow and the map of Austin. His brow knit together in confusion. He took it in. I met eyes with Rivkah, trying to communicate my panic. We had no plan for what to do if someone walked into our little warehouse.

"He's out in Bastrop. They keep finding empty graves, but they found children's clothes, bloody children's clothes," he continued, though I could tell he was trying to connect the dots of what he knew about me with what he was seeing now.

"Yeah, I was watching ..." I responded, trying to signal Rivkah in the hopes she could manufacture some excuse to get him out of here. She just looked at me wide eyed and panicked. Deceit wasn't her forte like it was mine. I turned towards Alex, thinking I would just offer to buy him breakfast so

I could get him out of the workshop, but he was already over at the map, his finger poking at the hole that arrow had left.

"This is where they found the house," he said, glancing at me.

I was ready. "Just keeping track, they said they hadn't found him yet, so I figured—"

"You were wearing that last night ... when I came to drop off the sample. You haven't changed or been home." His voice held accusation.

"Sometimes I just pick up whatever clothes are on the floor." I tried explaining.

"Even when those clothes have dirt and mud on them?" he countered. "I wanna make a bet that if I had that mud checked out, it would be the same sort of shit that's in the forest?"

Was he accusing me of hurting his little girl? Did he think I had done this?

He marched over to me. He was in my face, and for a moment, I thought he would just swing on me. He was giving that vibe a lot lately. "How did you find him? What did you find? Did you already kill him?" The questions came out of him rapid-fire.

To be honest, I was impressed. He had put the map and my clothes together and come up with the right answer extremely quickly. I held up my hands to give myself some space.

"No, I didn't kill him, I just found the place. He got the drop on me."

"So, he was out there ... and why didn't you call me? Why did you call them? Now I can't do shit about it. If you had called me before going out there, we could have taken him together, but now ... now he's fled and taken another little girl with him."

I could see Rivkah's eyes watching us, somewhere between worry and I told you so, but I couldn't deal with her at the moment.

"I didn't call you because I couldn't. And I'm glad I didn't, because if I had, you would be dead. I barely got out of there alive," I explained. "Look, the cops found blood out at the Bastrop place, his blood. I shot him, I put a bullet in his eye. It didn't stop him. It barely slowed him."

"Bullshit. You missed and thought you hit him because of the rain."

"No, I saw the ruined mess of his face, and I'm sure if you look into it, you'll find three shell casings, because I shot him three fucking times."

"That doesn't make any sense," he protested.

I spread my arms wide. "What do you see here? What do you think I'm doing?"

Alex stared me down for a few more seconds before he turned, looking around the warehouse. Rivkah shot me a panicked look—I think she realized what I was about to do.

"I don't know, crafts. It looks like you're making jewelry?" He was at a loss.

"Ze'ev." Rivkah murmured my name. She didn't want to get thrown in the loony bin. Probably didn't want to see me get thrown there either.

"You've seen me in the middle of a lot of shit, Alex. I've brought you evidence, I called to report crimes in progress ... I was the one who alerted the cops to those two cultists in Round Rock."

Alex looked at me, confusion on his face. Not real confusion, but the sort of mental dissonance of someone who sees the answer staring them in the face but doesn't want to accept it.

"You asked how Mullhani got those burns on his face," I said. "You wondered how I got embroiled with a bunch of cultists. Hell, y'all are still trying to sort out what was going on there. Well now I'm just telling you."

"What are you trying to say, Zev?" Alex asked.

"That those cultists were necromancers, and the thing I shot in the forests of Bastrop wasn't human."

✡

It took us a while to hash everything out with Alex. I don't know if he was more receptive to the idea because if something inhuman took his daughter, then he didn't have to lose all faith in humanity. Or maybe he had seen enough weird shit in the last year to be open minded. Whatever the case, he didn't call an ambulance of men in white clothes to pick me up. That was the good news.

I made everyone more coffee, and we spent the morning explaining the basics of who I actually was and what I actually did to Alex. It was a lot for anyone to take in for sure, but the fact was now that he had all the pieces of the puzzle, the picture finally made sense. Not that having a clear picture would help him at all; ignorance, after all, is bliss. Revealing the hidden world to a person carries risks. Risks that have a lot to do with a person's age. Like with Sandy, her risk in being exposed was becoming visible to those things that normally stayed hidden from human sight. For someone like Alex, it had more to do with his mental health.

You didn't just get to learn that your entire understanding of the world was flawed and walk away without some mental dissonance. And he was going through enough strain as it was. I'm not sure why I told him, I'm not sure I did the right thing. All I know is that telling someone the truth felt like a huge unburdening to my soul. One less person in the world I needed to lie to. I fessed up to the crimes I had committed while in pursuit of stopping worse things. I explained the real danger of Basken, and, finally, I explained why we believed the man in the woods had been—and I still had trouble believing this myself—a werewolf.

He looked dazed at the end of it all. I didn't blame him. He sat, head in hands, staring at the ground.

"You're telling me a lot of insane things, Ze'ev," he finally said quietly. He sounded defeated.

"Yeah. The world's even crazier than you thought."

"So, stopping Hayley's killer is impossible." He sounded so nihilistic in that moment, it was heartbreaking.

"No. Not impossible, it just requires more finesse. It requires a bit more planning and specialized knowledge and tools. But it is possible, and I will do it," I promised, though I had no idea how I would.

I locked eyes with Rivkah. She was probably hearing the death knell of sleepless nights of research.

She nodded her agreement. "We will."

Chapter 10

When Alex finally left the warehouse, his visit had costs us most of the day. I wasn't angry, though; like I said, it was a blessing that we didn't have to deal with hiding the truth from Alex anymore. Rivkah was off to pick up Sandy and bring her back to the lab. We were going to start her informal education into the world of the weird. It seemed so trifling a thing to do when we had so much big and terrible other crap to deal with, but it wasn't really trifling at all.

I sat at my desk looking over notes and handouts I had printed about various holy books, almost feeling like a real teacher. Magical knowledge and religious knowledge, at least in my world, collided. Sometimes those junctures were smooth and made some sort of logical sense. Sometimes those collisions broke with traditional teachings in painful, jarring ways. There were also the needs of the student to consider.

I had taught Rivkah alchemy and the mystic sciences first. It's what she would be good at but also what would help her dive fully into the world of the mythic. That had been an easy call. What the hell was I going to teach a high school girl? I had originally planned to hash it out with Rivkah, see what the girls had talked about, what sparked her interest, and what would keep these lessons from being pure drudgery. Alex had sort of killed that plan by showing up. There were, of course, the building blocks of mystic thought, those basic tenets and theories on which all other action was built. But those building blocks required good foundations in theology. And not just Jewish theology. Sure, Judaism was the basis for my, and I assumed Sandy's, belief, but Judaism was only 6000 years old or so; the world and some of the things in it were much, much older. Specifically, the Sheydim. In order for Sandy to understand them, she would need to delve outside the view of our own faith, at least some.

I had print outs from books of fairy myths from around the world. Faeries, demons, spirits. Normally I wouldn't dive into the Sheydim first, I would start with dybbukim, human ghosts, and spirits. But with what Nathan had said about the things stalking Sandy, I needed to hit the ground running.

Finally, the door opened and the girls walked in. I pushed all the papers into a manila folder and stood, meeting them before they could come all the way in.

"Actually, we're going for a ride, Sandy."

"We are?"

"You are?" Rivkah echoed, surprised.

"Yep, Rivkah here needs to focus on researching our little canine problem, and I need to get out for a bit, stretch my legs." I grinned as best I could and winked at Rivkah as I passed. "Rapid regeneration at least, maybe silver will work?" I was joking, mostly. The truth was I had no idea what would or wouldn't work on a goddamn werewolf.

Sandy trailed after me as I walked out of the lab

and got into my car.

✡

I drove without much of a destination in mind. I started with some basic chit-chat, how was she liking Austin, what about the school, what had she and Rivkah done already? After a few moments, I ran out of kid friendly conversation and we sat in silence. Sandy slowly flipped through the handouts I had printed for her.

"Mr. Kaplan?" She sounded nervous.

"Yeah?"

"I can't read Hebrew that well ... I mean I know the letters, I can sound it out, but I can't understand any of this."

I glanced at the papers I had printed. Some of it was in Hebrew, I hadn't considered that. Usually by the time someone came to me, they were fluent in at least Hebrew, or maybe I was just used to working with Rivkah, who admittedly was an outlier on the intelligence scale.

"That's okay, I'll explain everything," I assured her. "Nathan told me you had been seeing ... things." I didn't want to put thoughts in her head until I had real information.

"Yeah," she answered quietly.

"Like the man in your mirror?" I pressed.

She shook her head. "No, when he came, he was just there. You know? But now, I'm seeing things in the shadows, or I was back home. I haven't seen them here yet. But they look like people. But I can tell they aren't. I see them all the time. When I'm with other people, I can see them in the crowds or in the distance; but when I'm alone, I feel like they creep closer." She paused, and I could hear the fear in her voice. "I don't know what they want, but I feel like they're closing in. I was afraid to go to sleep because I know they knew where I lived, and what if they decided to come into my room? What if they decide to go after my parents?"

I nodded. I remembered the way the monsters congregated. I saw what Nathan had meant when he said typical Sheydim behavior. Intensely dangerous creatures if pissed off, unfathomable behavior.

"Well, I doubt you have anything to worry about, it's unlikely there's any malice in them. You aren't old enough to have done anything to piss them off." I grinned, trying to communicate that she should feel comfortable. But I knew my smiles were never the most comforting thing in the world. "My guess is that they're just curious. Your brush with the dybbuk in the mirror marked you. Think of it as sort of a brightly colored paint. Suddenly, you stand out from other people to things like them. They don't want to hurt you, they're just trying to figure who and what you are. Once they figure that out, they'll mostly ignore you."

"What are they?" she asked, flipping through the papers in her lap as though it might contain the answer.

"So, before I tell you that, I need to explain the difference between Mythic belief, faith, Aggadah, and religion." I smiled when she rolled her eyes; I knew exactly how she felt. "Religion for us is Judaism, right? It's the rules, the Torah, the culture, the life cycle. Religion is how we engage in our faith, whether or not we completely agree with the religion."

"Right, that's why so many people say they're spiritual but not religious."

"Exactly. They have faith, but they don't have a neat box to put that faith in. A lot of those people borrow aspects from various religions, and that's fine, faith is personal, religion is, generally speaking, communal. But we have the Torah and all of our holy literature. Stuff written by people who didn't know or understand science, people with agendas."

Sandy nodded. It was something most non-fundamentalists talked about, so I knew the language wouldn't be completely alien to her.

"Mythic belief is the supernatural aspects of religion and faith. Our mythology, things like angels, and nephilim, and all the things that can't or at least haven't been explained by science. These things we can often chalk up to the authors not understanding science."

"Okay, but what about the dybbuk? Where is the scientific explanation for that?"

"I'm getting to that," I chided her, but I could see she was interested. She had those wide curious eyes. I remembered seeing her curiosity when I performed the exorcism. I remembered thinking it was a dangerous thing but one of my favorite things about kids. "Finally, we have aggadah, our folktales, our mythology, our stories that we dismiss as being apocryphal or allegorical. Sometimes they are, sometimes they aren't. And the truth is ..." I paused, trying to find the words even though I had spoken about this before, even though, so far, this was my entire life's work.

"The truth is something that lies between all of those points. We can't extricate the truth from the myth. Some things don't make sense, and some things we know seem to contradict other things we have accepted as fact. The Sheydim come from our oldest stories. They come from trying to understand the world and trying to figure out our place in it. Do you know Bereshit?"

She nodded slightly. "Genesis, the first book of Torah."

"Right, what order are things created in?" I

asked.

She fell silent, trying to recall how things were made in the myth of creation. "Um, light, the skies and the ocean, land, plants …" She was counting on her fingers, trying to remember. I was actually already impressed. I would have probably accepted a noncommittal shrug. She paused, struggling to remember past the third day.

"The celestial bodies are next, sun, stars, and moon, and then on day five we have all the animals, and on day six we have mankind." I filled in the blanks. "But there's so much more, and in the Talmud and Mishnah, we question when and where other things came into being. For instance, angels and the Sheydim."

She watched me, a rapt pupil. I think she was just hoping I would stop talking about the bible and start talking about monsters.

"Are angels real?" she asked.

"We'll … we'll cover angels some other time, okay? Now, according to aggadah, the Sheydim were meant to be humans. They were halfway through the act of being created when the sun went down on the sixth day, which brought about the first Shabbot, the first sabbath, the first day of rest. And so the Sheydim were left unfinished. Now in Torah study, people will talk about how this was done purposefully as to show how important Shabbot is, that even HaShem pauses their work in order to observe it."

"That seems … I don't know, that seems like a weak explanation," Sandy muttered, worried about blasphemy.

"Agreed. While we show HaShem resting in the Torah, the truth is the act of creation and physics and the laws of nature never rest, so why would this happen? The Sheydim are humanity's cousins, in a way, if we follow the aggadah. They were created after us, but they weren't us, not completely. They share traits with angels: supernatural powers, terrifying appearances, and immortality. But they also share things with us: our appetites, our humanity, and our free will." I paused to let her take that in.

"You don't make them sound all that bad," she said finally. "But Nathan made it sound like I was in danger."

"Well, think of it like this, Sandy. The Sheydim act with almost no oversight. They don't answer to the police or the government, they have superpowers, and they are just like people; some are good and kind. Some ..." I trailed off.

Sandy sat in silence, processing this new information. I imagined she was thinking about what she would do if she had that freedom and those powers. That or she was wondering why the Sheydim didn't take over and rule humanity. I let her think about what I said before pulling into a drive-thru to grab some dinner. We ordered and sat in silence waiting for our food.

"So." She finally broke the quiet. "What do they want?"

"I don't know. They want different things, I suppose, just like us. They have their own government, their own nations. They have their own lives and jobs and, generally speaking, they rarely overlap with ours, to my knowledge."

She shot me a sharp look as I passed her burger to her and started driving again. I was heading west into the hill country of Bee Caves. I figured I could drive us somewhere we could watch the sunset and she could ask any questions I left her with.

"In the Talmud, there is a section about going into ruins and about how you should avoid going into them alone or just with someone of the opposite sex. The warnings are you could get robbed, someone might think you are being improper, or demons."

"Demons?" She seemed surprised to find out demons were mentioned in the Talmud.

"Demons. The Talmud is filled with supernatural elements. In fact, most of our understanding of the supernatural world can be found first in the Talmud. But the demons in this particular passage are *Mallikim* not Sheydim. I don't tend to think of the Sheydim as being demonic." I glanced at the papers in her lap before pulling off of highway 71 and pulling into the Bee Caves Whole Foods and parking. "Think of them like the Jewish version of faeries. They have courts, they are disparate and unique with politics and intrigue, but they aren't evil. Not in the sense that the Mallikim are."

Sandy looked like her mind was blown. She stared down at the papers, flipping through the various handouts like it would magically give her the answers, which in a way, I supposed was true. I was so focused on watching the gears turn in her head that I didn't notice the cop car that had pulled in behind us until it's flashing lights illuminated her face.

✡

Cursing, I looked in the rear view. Our old friend from the bus station, Officer Stevens, was getting out of the car. Mirrored shades hid the empty sockets of his eyes. I turned to Sandy and set my lips in a grim line.

"Stay here," I told her before getting out, ignoring her protest.

I shut the car door and turned to face the Sheyd. I wanted to ease her fears not stoke them. But this motherfucker wasn't playing by the rules. There were civilians inside the Whole Foods, we were in public. He walked calmly towards me, the manic too wide smile already plastered across his face.

I stopped about three meters from him. We stood there looking at each other.

"Generally speaking, you stay in your car when pulled over, Mr. Kaplan." He still spoke in the sing song voice.

"Generally speaking, cops have eyes, not little grubs," I answered.

He laughed and shrugged, taking a step forward, though he stopped as I reached into my pocket and gripped the talisman of warding on my keychain. Sheydim weren't spirits in the strictest sense, but they were close enough that invocations could affect them. His smile wavered a tad, but he shook his head.

"Believe it or not, Mr. Kaplan, I am not your enemy." Stevens raised his hands defensively. "I already told you I'm just a concerned on-looker." He tilted his head as if listening to someone. "Ah yes, and we did tell you last time to try to understand who your enemies are."

"Why don't you fucking enlighten me then, *Officer*." I sneered the word.

His smile fell away. "You have always been surrounded by the darkness, Ze'ev, but now the shadows grow thick with harmful and hateful things. Things boiling out of the void that are hungry. Hungrier than you can imagine." His smile returned full force as I heard the car door behind me open. Fuck.

"Sandy, get back in the car," I yelled, not taking my eyes off the Sheyd. I hated him using my name.

"Mr. Kaplan ..." Sandy sounded concerned, which wasn't too weird, considering.

"Sandy, get back in the car!" I ordered again.

"But what about them?" she asked.

Them? Both the *cop* and I turned our heads and saw that in the space of time we had been talking, a man had appeared and approached. He stood a respectful distance away. I recognized him, his big red beard was a dead giveaway, as was the wolf at his side. I had been right. He had my scent. His crazy smile mimicked Stevens's. I wondered if they were working together.

"Sandy! Get back in the fucking car!" I screamed.

Now the panic in my voice forced her to move, but everything was already happening at once.

The bearded ginger started towards her, his wolf headed for the Sheyd, and I ran to intercept the ginger. I bent over and didn't slow down as I plowed into the larger man. He didn't fall, but I slowed him enough for Sandy to get in the car and lock the door. She was screaming. I turned and glanced back at the Sheyd; he was dodging the wolf's teeth and lunges, the grin on his face now tight and dangerous.

My distraction was stupid. I felt his hand grab me by the neck. He lifted me off the ground with one damn hand and threw me. I hit the top of my car and rolled over it to collapse on the other side. I stood shakily, but already he was coming around the car at me.

"Didn't I shoot you?" I asked, backpedaling, as much to get him away from the car and Sandy as to put distance between us.

"Peter Stübbe ain't that easy to kill, you piece of shit."

Well, now I had a name. If I survived the night, that would be useful.

I reached for my holster and realized I wasn't carrying my gun. That was stupid of me. I had hardly left the house without it since the incident with Basken. But I had thought that since I was with Sandy, I would leave the sidearm in my desk at the warehouse. I continued to backpedal.

The sound of the wolf whimpering caused Peter to turn, concern on his big stupid face. I charged him while he was distracted, jumping at the last second to deliver a devastating punch to the back of his head. Or that was my intention. He turned when he heard me running and grabbed my arm, twisting and tossing me as easily as someone might toss a ragdoll. I bounced off a car, and the alarm started going off. I rose unsteadily to my feet and moved towards Peter again.

I needed to be more careful, he was stronger, faster, and also seemingly indestructible. I didn't really know what to make of all this. The supernatural world was rarely this open about their activities. The Sheyd had obviously grown complacent with his disguise, but Peter? I guessed he just felt invincible. Was that invincibility part of his nature or part of his spell work? Only one way to find out.

I went on the defensive as I met with Peter again, my hands up like a boxer, dodging between his punches and avoiding his grabs. When he over-extended, I threw a punch into his ribs and was rewarded with a little *oof* from him. At least I could hurt him. As I dodged and weaved around his punches and threw out my own counter attacks, I whispered the ancient names under my breath. A steady mantra of angelic identities. The air was growing thick with power. If they wanted the hidden world revealed, I was more than happy to oblige. I think the Sheyd realized what I was doing first, sensitive ears or maybe just more knowledgeable.

"Ze'ev, duck!"

It was weird hearing my name in something other than a threat. I kept my chant as I dropped to my hands and knees. The dead body of the massive wolf flew over my head and slammed into Peter, bowling him over. Peter rose, gathering the limp animal in his arms. It was obvious its spine was broken in several places from the way it hung unnaturally. He howled his rage and pulled something out of his pocket, a talisman, and held it against the canine. He waited a second and then lifted it and pressed it against the wolf again. Nothing happened.

I rose to my feet.

"Your magic isn't going to work here. Not now." Around us, unseen to me or Peter, angels sapped the magic from the air, stealing the bits of power and energy that Peter's amulet was attempting to use to heal the wolf. It answered my question. His unnatural healing was fueled by some sort of witchcraft. Powerful shit too, more powerful than Basken had been if he was able to bring the wolf back to true life.

Peter looked up. He was no longer smiling, he no longer looked like he was having a good time. I had hoped the looming threat of mortality would scare him off, but he just looked furious. He set his wolf down, touched its neck tenderly, then launched himself past me and at the Sheyd. Stevens fell back against his own car, his shades falling as he was tackled. The thing that lived in his socket scrambled out and latched onto Peter, its numerous little bladed legs scratching and tearing at the Ginger's face and neck in furious motion. It was scalping him, no, flaying him alive. But even as I watched, his face was knitting itself back together. My invocation of angels still held; this wasn't a spell, this was just Peter.

Peter reached up, grabbing the scrabbling thing and crushed it in his hand. Ichor and screams leaked from his hand, dripping down as it died. Stevens looked distraught for a moment and then

… simply vanished. One moment he was there, the next he, and his car, were gone.

I didn't stick around to watch and see what would happen next. I ran and threw myself into my car as quickly as I could, throwing it in drive and speeding off. Sheydim could become unseen at will. Apparently, he had decided that an unkillable monster was above his paygrade when harassing me and Sandy.

Sandy was still screaming, but she was screaming questions. She was in full panic mode. First lesson was going to have to be how to stay calmer than that. I glanced over at her. Her eyes were rolling in animal fright.

"You're okay; we're okay."

She looked at me. She was already starting to cry.

I reached over and squeezed her shoulder. "We're okay."

"What was that? Why did that man attack us?! Was that a Sheyd?" She kept asking questions, but I needed to focus on driving.

I had taken off down 71, but turned onto 620 towards Lakeway. I could take a big loop around Austin and head back into town fairly close to Rivkah's place. We were in the wealthiest area in the Austin area now, and I needed to concentrate. I didn't think the Sheyd would actually come after me again tonight, but getting pulled over by an actual cop would give the damned Peter plenty of opportunity to catch up with me. So I drove the speed limit and obeyed traffic laws. Difficult to do when your adrenaline is pumping and a teenage girl is screaming questions at you.

I stayed outwardly calm, and eventually, Sandy stopped shouting at me.

"What was that?" Her question trembled in the air.

"The cop is a Sheyd who has been following me for a few days. The other man ..." I paused, trying to think about the best way to explain to this young woman that I had taken on myself to go against an insane magic-using immortal child murderer. "The other man is what Rivkah stayed behind to research. You remember me suggesting silver?" I glanced over at her, and she was glaring at me.

"Are you saying ..." she started and then shook her head, obviously not wanting to voice the stupid question. "Are you saying that man was a fucking werewolf?"

I wanted to reprimand her for her language, well, no I didn't. But I felt like I should. "Maybe. We're still trying to figure out what he is."

"Werewolves are just pretend," Sandy said firmly.

"Maybe; the last werewolf we have actual accounts of was from the Baal Shem Tov, who killed a werewolf that was threatening the children of his village. Listen, Sandy, I would have been happy if you could have gone your entire life without encountering any of this. I don't wish this knowledge or life on anyone, but that option's been taken from you. I'm sorry, one thing we never get to say is that something is just pretend."

"But why was it taken from me? That's not fair! I didn't do anything wrong." She was on the verge of tears again.

"Yeah, I know, that's the shittiest part. Once we encounter the supernatural, we become sort of a beacon to them. That's why the Sheydim have been following you and watching you. If an angry ginger werewolf is the weirdest thing you encounter in your life, count your blessings, there is plenty of weirder, scarier shit out there."

"Like what?" She had a bit of a challenge in her voice, and I had to smile. Her curiosity outweighed her fear, probably outweighed everything for her. She and Rivkah would be best friends before the end of the school year. Assuming I survived it.

"Later," I said. She wanted everything at once, but knowing about the fae creatures that were following both of us seemed more pertinent than anything else at the moment. "For now, let's focus on the Sheydim."

Chapter 11

Sandy was dropped off, Rivkah was home, Sara was at work. I went by her place and walked Toof. He was a good dog for a rotund idiot. He had cost Sara an arm and a leg in medical expenses, mostly due to him eating things that weren't food. I was a little leery on my walk; being outdoors alone, even in a neighborhood like this, made me feel exposed. But that wasn't Toof's fault. We walked around the block, enjoying the night air.

It's a pity, I think, that I can't just enjoy these nights anymore. There's always some bullshit coming at me, making me afraid. It reminded me of the PTSD I had seen from soldiers who had spent too much time in active warzones. It gets to where you can't turn it off. They call it paranoia, but at some point, it was necessary for survival. I was lucky I could still count my enemies and the entities that wanted to hurt or kill me on the fingers of one hand.

Basken was a mad man, a necromancer and serial killer who had thrown everything he could against me, from attempting to frame me for murder to summoning a damn ghost through my phone. He was a man who had studied a very specific brand of magic, one that involved lots of gestures and chanting, so I had cut the tendons in his hand and stopped his magic slinging days for at least a while. But Basken was in jail, and so were several members of his cult. Members who may have the skill to heal or repair the damage I caused. I was hopeful that the night I led a pack of furious ghouls into the necromancers' midst would be the last time I had to deal with him. But I wasn't confident.

Speaking of ghouls, there was Mr. Grin and Baalrachius. Those two had been prominent figures in my nightmares since I met them. Ghouls were feral humanoid creatures that bore resemblance to an emaciated hyena that stood on two legs. Most of them I had met or had dealings with were scavengers who wore rags and broke into cemeteries to feast on dead bodies. Monstrous creatures, but ones I had an uneasy truce with until Basken got them all riled up. Baalrachius, the self-styled 'king of ghouls,' had ordered my execution. If not for the double dealings of Mr. Grin, who seemed to be some high-ranking assassin in the world of monsters, I would probably be dead.

Mr. Grin had decided I could be used to further his ends and was the one who had been sending me texts sending me on wild goose chases to hunt down rare and evil tomes and artifacts. I had another one from him now. As soon as I dropped Toof back off, I would check that out. Now that I had a moment to breathe in between being followed by Sheydim and being attacked by various entities, I could spend a little energy trying to figure out what this latest chore was. I'm sure he thought I was gathering these books to give to him, but the truth was these books needed to be off the street, out of reach of anyone who would actually use them. I just hadn't figured out how to deal with Grin yet.

That left me with Peter Stübbe. The immortal. The witch. The werewolf. The child murdering psychotic immortal werewolf witch that had attacked me in public. I took a deep breath, watching Toof snorfle at some bushes, trying to find an interesting scent with his brachycephalic nose. Peter broke the rules, in my opinion. Most things either used magic or were magic. Sure, the angels and the Sheydim seemed perfectly capable of either, but I had never actually seen either sort of being use magic beyond their natural abilities. This thing, Peter, was both. Or was he?

I needed more information. I needed to figure out what he was. Was he actually a werewolf? Or was he just a man who had stumbled upon spellwork that gave him inhuman abilities? Too many questions made my job more dangerous than it had to be. But as of yet, I didn't know how to find the answers to any of them. I supposed the first thing I would do once I got back to the lab was research Peter's name. He had spoken with a bit of a Polish accent, one I was used to from dealing with Beit Din representatives. That gave me just enough information to probably find nothing at all. Especially if he had always lived so far off the grid. But it was better than nothing, and I still had the hair sample. I had assumed after I found him in the forest, he would have warded himself from being found again, but there was no harm in trying.

I took Toof back home and fed him, kneeling down to hug the rugged ball of fat and wrinkles. I didn't get to spend nearly as much time as I would like with animals, and Toof always helped bring me back to a calmer, happier place. He ignored me; he was a very food driven beast. I chuckled, watching him for a moment before rising and heading out the door.

✡

Once I was back in my car, it was time to get to work. The vehicle had essentially become my traveling office over the last few months. I had cleaned out the front seat for Sandy, but the back seat was still filled with papers, copies, and folders filled with research. How I missed the days of waltzing into a stranger's house and yelling at their mirror until a dybbuk went away. I grabbed the burner phone out of my glove compartment. I don't know how Grin had found the number, but that's where he had been sending his little orders. Powering it on, I scrolled through the text messages. There weren't that many, so I found the text from Grin pretty quickly. It simply read.

Esuriit et Mortuus Est - Johann Velk

Any other situation and I would have headed to Ancient Mysteries and talked to Amanda, they had a pretty good line on old and sometimes forbidden texts. But they also had a reason to *want* those texts. They were of the mind that there was no such thing as black magic, only practitioners who misused spellwork. I disagreed. Some magic was evil by its very nature. Like necromancy. I didn't have the time or patience to argue with or fight with Amanda on why she should give up ancient texts to me to hoard and keep from seeing the light of day. Luckily, I do have a couple of other options.

The Beit Din frowned on interspecies interactions. And after my truce with the ghouls had fallen apart, I guess I could see the wisdom behind that policy. I wondered how they would feel about the interfaith work I engaged in. My guess is that it would have varied from person to person, based on personal experience and personal faith. I wondered what sort of administrator I would be once I retired from active duty. I laughed to myself as I threw the car into drive and headed down to Cherry Creek in South Austin.

The truth was I didn't expect to retire. Not really. I expected to get killed in the line of duty. That wasn't a new idea. I had been prepared to die in the line of duty since I had encountered the Alukah in Jerusalem. It just hadn't been so likely until this last year. A lot of the Beit Din's leadership were retired exorcists. But there were far too few hunters that made it long enough to put down the gun and pick up the pen. I had made it my personal mission to make sure none of the trainees they sent to me followed my path.

Eventually, Nathan would probably send me a go-getter soldier, someone whose dream it was to hunt monsters and who I couldn't dissuade. They would die, they would get killed violently. And Nathan would ensure their death was covered up by pretty lies that would leave their family unsatisfied and empty. I wanted no part in that. I wondered if the lies for my death were already in place. If Nathan would simply push a button or make a call and cover up the existence of one of his oldest friends.

I was getting bitter. Maybe it was because I was doing this clandestine bullshit, maybe it was because my allies dwindled and my enemies grew. Now I needed to pay a call to an old friend.

I pulled up to the Cherry Creek strip mall. Cherry Creek wasn't the bad part of town, but it wasn't exactly the good part of town either. Nice small houses and dirt cheap section 8 apartments butted up against one another over here. This particular shopping center contained a thrift shop, an outreach church, a dog salon, a nail salon, narcotics anonymous, alcoholics anonymous, and a tattoo shop with a single artist. I could see the empty waiting room behind the hand painted window reading Firefly Tattoos, a nod to the serenity pledge that the AA people would be taking. In the waiting room, there was a large black cello, a couple of portfolio books to showcase the artist's work, and a shrine to Santa Muerte. A printed sign taped to the door reminded patrons that they could call to make an appointment and that sessions were by appointment only.

I should have called. Claeton, the artist inside, may not be inside; hell, he may not even be in Texas. Occasionally, he was flown to another part of the country by a client to continue the 'good work'. Too late now, I rang the *Ring* doorbell and waited a few moments. The lights were on, which meant he was probably in. But I knew that sometimes he left those on to give the less desirable elements of Cherry Creek the impression that he was home. Not that anyone who had a brain in their head would rob or steal from Jon Claeton.

Jon pushed open the door from the shop to the waiting room and gave a big grin when he saw me standing there. He was about 6'7", built like a linebacker, and covered in tattoos. His blue eyes shown with an energy men half his age couldn't muster. He swung the door open and grabbed my hand before pulling me forward into a half hug that nearly engulfed and crushed me. When he released me, I offered a grin and stepped past him into the shop.

Guitars lined the walls, each one customized. To the right was his office and reception desk, to the left, the room he actually did tattoos in. The rest of the shop was set up as a living area, a few chairs, a big TV with video games hanging off it, and then a back room with shelves where Jon made tactical armor for fun. Jon wasn't exactly a prepper, but he wasn't exactly not a prepper either. His two favorite maxims were 'it's better to be a warrior in a garden than a gardener in a war' and 'a well-armed society is a polite society'. I didn't see any guns, but I knew from experience that he kept handguns in at least four easy to reach locations, an AR latched under the reception desk, and a shotgun under the couch. All loaded, all ready. Like I said, anyone who tried to rob Jon was insane. Hell, I was probably safer here than in my own home. Jon was a good guy. He wanted Texas to secede and was an incorrigible troll who hated all politicians and anyone who backed any politician with near maniacal madness, but he also fought racism and anti-Semitic behavior wherever he saw it.

"What's up, Wolf? We finally going to get some ink on you?" he asked.

I chuckled and looked over at him.

"Your name is Wolf, you fight monsters, you need a bad-ass wolf tattoo."

"My name is Ze'ev."

"Yeah, which means wolf."

I rolled my eyes. A few of my southern friends called me Wolf instead of my actual name. It never really bothered me, some of them just couldn't get the Hebrew name past their lips. Jon could, he just thought Wolf was more bad-ass.

"Not today, unfortunately, business call."

"Yeah, and tattoos are my business," he countered.

"I know, I know." I raised my hands in defeat. "But I'm here for my business. I need some help."

"Yeah, I figured. You aren't the sort to come by unless you need something," he said as he grabbed a steel guitar off the wall and sat down heavily in an old leather recliner.

His words stung a little, they mirrored words I had heard from Amanda at Ancient Mysteries in the not too distant past. I sat in one of the rolling office chairs and listened while he noodled on the instrument. He was a good musician, though sometimes when you wanted to talk to him, he would just grab a guitar and stare at you while you waited for him to finish playing so you could talk.

"I get that a lot," I said, raising my voice over the sound of the strumming. "What do you know about werewolves?"

"Werewolves?" Jon stopped playing, looking at me like I was insane, which I suppose wasn't all that surprising. After a few seconds of Jon thinking while he plucked at the strings of his guitar, he rose and put the guitar back, stroking his chin with tattoo covered hands. "I guess it depends. Are we talking, like, Skin-Walkers? Old European myths? I mean, shit, Wolf, werewolf stories are a dime a dozen. Don't you have stuff you can pull from?"

"I don't know, man, I guess I'll try to find silver bullets?" Something about Jon's presence set me at ease, always did. I think it was the deep Texan that ran through him that I just felt familiar with. He was as covered in tattoos as Rivkah, big, and volatile, but he felt familiar.

"Nah, silver can't stand up to the strain you would put on a bullet, but ..." Jon mused before grinning slightly maniacally. "What you need is a blunderbuss!"

"Excuse me? Am I fighting Blackbeard now? Why would I want a blunderbuss?" I was trying to follow his logic but was at a loss.

"Look, maybe not a blunderbuss, but you take a shotgun shell, empty it out, and replace the buckshot with links from a silver chain or bits of silver shavings, and then ..." He pantomimed lifting a shotgun and taking a shot. It was brilliant, really, and not just for this. I could see making shotgun shells for all kinds of different monsters and boogymen. Jon sometimes said insanely weird, dumb shit, and sometimes he made me feel incredibly stupid.

"That ... is brilliant," I finally said. "I mean, assuming silver can actually stop him from healing, it's brilliant."

"So you've already met and thrown down with this werewolf? Is it a Nazi werewolf?" Jon was sitting up a little straighter. He was always ready to rumble into some sort of altercation; sobriety left him itching for a fight, looking for distraction from cravings. "Because I could probably get together some shells and ..."

I lifted my hand to stop him. "He's not a Nazi, just a menace, killed a few people." I didn't want to give him the full story; if he knew the truth, he would be out the door and riding his motorcycle into the woods of Bastrop to get torn apart. It was sort of a miracle he had survived this long. "But I do need to stop him. Like I said, I don't know about the whole silver thing. I shot him with normal bullets, blew a hole in his head. It just ..." I made motions with my hands trying to pantomime a head coming back together.

"Damn." He sat back down and stared off into space before reaching for a small glass pipe. I waited patiently while he lit the pipe and took in a great lungful of smoke. He held it there, then slowly breathed out a cloud of smoke and offered me the pipe. I took the pipe and looked it over, tempted, but then the idea of being sluggish when I ran into trouble again made me set it down unsmoked.

"I mean, it sounds dangerous," he said. "Whatever you bring, you need to make sure it can finish the job."

I nodded my agreement. I would filter away the shotgun idea for another day. He was right, next time I met up with Peter, whenever that was, I needed to finish this.

"Actually, there is something else," I said finally.

"A book?" he asked, the haze of marijuana's embrace drooping his eyelids. He had said it increased his mojo, his connection to the spirit world. I didn't know if that were true or not. Maybe a spirit told him I was looking for a book, or maybe it was just a very obvious guess.

"A book," I confirmed. I pulled my phone out and thumbed to the text message from Grin before passing it over.

He took it in his massive hands—the phone looked like a kid's toy in his grip.

He read the words and then leaned back, thinking about it. "I think I can help. I've heard of Velk, a lot of people who are obsessed with Crowley talk about Velk. Velk's not easy to find, though. Most of his books were only done through small runs." Jon, despite his tattooed biker appearance (mostly due to him being a biker tattoo artist), had amassed an incredible collection of rare and obscure tomes. He could have probably lived quite comfortable by just selling off a few of the books in his library. I had to wonder what he thought of me going after increasingly dangerous books.

"Velk was an occultist," Jon said, "I mean, obviously, but his entire practice and belief was all about locating and binding beings from outside our dimension to his will. He called them the Uber-Alptraum, sort of like a suped-up demonic fae." He handed the phone back to me.

"Sounds like the Sheydim to me," I said before rising to my feet. "If you can find me a copy, I would be grateful."

He leaned forward on his knees, nodding slightly. "Any chance you can get me a date with Rivkah?" He grinned. He didn't actually want to date her, he wanted to sleep with her. He liked Jewish women, he liked Jewish women enough that three of his kids, spread across a few mothers, were Jewish. Two of them were Marines now, certified badasses. I figured it was only a matter of time before the Beit Din got their talons in the boys and asked me to train new hunters. Not that they would need training; with Jon as their dad and the training marines get, they would probably be able to train me.

I smiled in response to his request. "I'm not a Shidduch, Jon, but I'll mention you would like to see her." I offered my hand, but he knocked it away, standing himself to engulf me in a bear hug, then setting me down.

"All right, man, let's go shooting together soon, and I'll catch you up with where I am on your Velk, deal?"

"Sounds good, Jon, take care of yourself until then." I headed out the door and back into the warm night air.

No calls, no messages. For a moment, there was peace.

Chapter 12

I went home. I didn't live that far from Cherry Creek, and I had completed all my chores. I mean, other than tracking down a book of damned extra-planar magic, killing a werewolf, and preparing a teenage girl to fight the forces of evil. Other than that, I had done everything I needed to do. I stopped by the taco truck on my way—I eat a lot of tacos.

I pushed open the door to my apartment, and my fingers twitched as I faced the darkness of my own home. There had been too many surprises here in the last year to feel completely at ease here. Another reason I had taken to sleeping in my car so often.

When nothing came out of the dark to attack me, I let out a breath I had been holding and set my keys down on the side table. I then made my way into the living room to eat my dinner, flicking the TV on to watch some mindless cooking competition show. It was just noise. Noise that eased the painful burden silence brought by forcing me to be alone with my own thoughts. I sat there, staring at the TV, watching Alton Brown yelling about Morimoto's rice, and chuckling at the secret ingredients for a while. But after an hour, it was late. I shut off the TV and poured myself a glass of whiskey. Setting the glass down on the table, I pulled out my tallit and teffilim.

I wasn't as religious as Nathan, I had seen too much to think that all the answers could be found in a single faith. I knew there were monsters and beings that defied my understanding of the world. But I had yet to find a path other than Judaism that made me happy. Maybe it was just my upbringing or my friends in the community. But, for better or worse, I was Jewish and had no intention of abandoning that. I stood in the kitchen and said my evening prayers, rocking on my feet while reciting the Maariv. The Amidah fell from my mouth in an easy cadence that could almost be a chant. Maybe my intention wasn't fully on the prayers I was uttering, but the prayers brought me comfort. They eased a burden in my heart, and for a moment, while wrapping myself in the trappings of faith and prayer, I could feel safe and secure. After I finished the Aleinu, I picked up my glass of whiskey and downed it before pulling off my religious trappings and heading to my bed. I didn't even get changed out of my clothes, just fell into my bed and into dreams.

✡

I stood in Bristol Texas, one of the microcosms of a city that was a stone's throw from Crisp, where I had spent so much of my youth and experienced so much of what would force me down the path I was on. Bristol didn't hold much in it beyond judgmental pastors and a gas station that advertised that it sold sushi. If you ever want to die of dysentery, go ahead and buy some sushi from a gas station in a town that most people who live near it have never heard of. I wasn't sure why I was in Bristol. I took a step, and the world blurred, and I was standing before my great-grandmother's grave. She was buried in Bristol along with the rest of the Penrods and most of the Gulledges. The north Texas winds were hot and pulled at my clothes as I stared down at Mittie's tombstone. She had been extremely Christian, and it had been hard at times. There was a friction caused by my mom catching her trying to teach us about Jesus. But despite her unwelcome proselytizing, she had been a kind woman to us. I took a step back away from the grave and the world shifted again.

I was in Crisp.

I didn't take another step. I knew this was a dream, it had to be. This dream and I were old companions, almost lovers with how many sweaty nights I had spent in this nightmare's embrace. The sun hung high over me, baking the paint off the facades of the small store and buildings of Crisp's main street. I knew where my next step would take me, and so I refused to take it. I wondered if I could out-wait my own psyche. I wondered if I had tried before. Dreams are strange things, and nightmares were strange and terrible.

In the Torah, dreams, visions, and reality merge and morph together to form prophecy or allegory. Patriarchs ascend ladders into heaven and wrestle with angels while chariots of fire hand down proclamations that may or may not be truly from the divine. Rabbinic sages have argued about the importance and meaning of dreams, and I personally knew at least three Jewish scholars who made a career from dream interpretation. It was something I hadn't looked into. That might seem insane with a dream I had at least once or twice a week, especially in my line of work, but I couldn't bring myself to do it. There was nothing positive to glean from this particular space and time. Nothing I wanted to dwell in.

I lifted my foot; against my will, I took the next step.

I stood outside the barn. The sun remained overhead. I could feel my skin burning, protesting the constant heat and rays. The barn offered shade, but it also offered everything I was terrified of and the event that had set me on a life path of pain and danger. The barn had grown with me, it remained as large to me now as it had when I was a child. I shook my head and moved to the massive doors of the barn. They were slightly ajar, as they always were.

I slipped into the darkness of the barn. The shadows inside were oppressive, but I knew they hid rusted farm equipment and old moldering hay. In the far corner, I saw the skeletal cow that was always there, terrifying as a child, less of an issue now. But the cow was different. It wasn't just old bones. No, there was the gossamer of desiccated flesh and stretched taut tendons that lay over it like a shroud. Somehow, this small changed detail hurt my stomach, wrenching it into a tight ball of fear.

I swallowed, reaching back for the door, but my hand only encountered the solid rotting wood wall of the barn. The shadows grew, and I realized there was movement in those shadows. Great hunched shapes moving in the murk, eyes that reflected light at disconcerting angles flashed as they watched me. At first, I only saw the one, then two, then more. The stink of wet dog reached my nose, and I realized all of the shapes in the shadows were wolves.

"They are at the door, so to speed Ze'ev ben Daveed." A voice as strong as steel that sounded like a whisper in a hurricane from miles away.

I turned to find an old man, emaciated with pallid skin stretched like someone was tanning albino leather on his bare bones. He was dressed in an immaculate black suit with a wilted and dead tulip pinned to his lapel. He smiled, showing the yellowed teeth of a rotting skull behind lips that looked like they would tear at the slightest stretch. Despite his horrifying and alien appearance, he looked somehow familiar to me, as though I knew him. As though he had stood here, with me, before.

"Who are you?" It was a pertinent question. I understood this was a dream, but I had never seen this man before. Why was he intruding on my dreams? Why was he a part of a nightmare that had been my constant companion for as long as I could remember?

I felt tense, my brain sluggishly trying to process the possibility of things that could invade a man's nightmares. Most of them were pretty nasty.

"Be not afraid, Ze'ev, but they *are* at the doors, and so are you," he said.

I glanced away from him and found myself at the back door of the barn. Though there was the true terror, the true nightmare. I could feel the shadows pressing in, growing closer, as though the sunbeams that punctured the rotted roof were growing less powerful in this frozen time. With the shadows came the wolves. The horrible old man placed a skeletal thin hand on my shoulder. I wanted to recoil, but I was locked in place, as frozen in place as the particles of dust were suspended in the beams unmoving.

"You come here, almost nightly, seeking to undo the past. Seeking to change the forks of time. You cannot, you will not. Doubt and regret choke you and keep you compressed into a single point of pain instead of achieving what you could. You will not tamper with time or the past. Your choices are made. Your life set on the path you have embarked on. You think, if not you then another, but there is no other for these tasks. HaShem sets us on our missions, our cycles, our lives."

"Why me?" I asked, my voice echoing into the shadows of the barn, drawing out growls from unseen wolves. "Why do I have to be the one to face down all the nightmares the world throws at me?"

"Oh, Ze'ev," his horrible creaking voice answered, softened just a hint as though in sadness—though I doubted his terrible face was capable of expressing much of anything. "You are not tasked with healing and saving your world, but neither are you free from the obligation to do what you can." He released my shoulder and pressed something into my hand. Something heavy and cold as death. I couldn't even look down to see what was in my hand; I didn't know if I even wanted to. "You think yourself capable of bucking the system, but you are dust, Ze'ev." He gestured to the door in front of us. "But all of this, this universe, it was made for you."

Tendrils were pushing through the cracks in the door, through the openings. The tentacles looked like some beast that had been turned inside out, dripping viscera from pulsing veins. Along the length of the dripping limbs, eyes opened, each one rolling wildly. When one would land on me, it would stop and glare, full of malice and hate. Mouths filled with jagged and alien teeth tore through from under the flesh of the tendrils and howled at me. I didn't have a choice. Maybe I did at some point, but the horrible old man was right, this choice had already been made.

I opened the door and stepped into the embrace of the waving tentacles. From the shadows, Kristine's face emerged and screamed my name before two stone hands appeared from the darkness and crushed her in a shower of gore.

✡

I jolted up in bed, still dressed. My clothes were soaked through with a cold, clammy sweat. Nightmares. Already the memory of the nightmare was fading. That was all right; I could guess what it had been. The barn. That fucking barn. I didn't know why it wouldn't let me go. But that was the nature of dreams. I glanced at the clock on my dresser; it was too early to really do anything. I rubbed my face and slowly stood up. Something slid off my leg and hit the floor with a dull thud. I bent over and picked it up. It was a disk of silver with Hebrew inscribed on both sides. On one side it said *I was made from dust,* and on the other, *The Universe was made for me.* I mouthed the words as I read them. It was a common enough phrase made popular by Chassids.

A common motto to remind people to stay humble and remember that all power and all things came from G-d, but also to realize the importance and power we had to act in a world that was created in part for us. I don't know that I agreed, I wasn't a fan of self-importance. I rolled the disk across my knuckles, considering where the hell it could have come from. I flipped it into the air like a coin, caught it, and smirked at the *I was made from dust* that looked up at me. Probably a gift from my mom or one of my sisters.

I tossed the disk back on my bed and stretched. I needed a shower; my clothes were still sticking to me. I also needed a plan. I could research Peter, that was a first step, seeing what the Internet could tell me. I could also make a list of shotgun shells I wanted to make. I wanted to kiss Claeton for the suggestion and also punch him in his big dumb face for waiting so long to make it. I smiled, crafting custom shotgun shells and organizing them was the sort of activity I would enjoy, something to bring some joy back into my life. Even if I never got to use them, it was such a cool little idea that it would be fun.

Instead of taking a shower immediately, which I should have done, I sat down and opened my little laptop. Rivkah hated the thing, said it was a relic of a bygone era. And that I was, in fact, a luddite for not upgrading. But the truth was it handled all the administrative functions I needed it to, spreadsheets and word docs, and it could surf the Internet just fine. And so I resisted buying a new laptop, despite the fact that I could probably expense it. I opened a spreadsheet and started making notes about what sort of things I could and couldn't fill a shotgun shell with. There were plenty of herbs and some metals that had a detrimental effect on supernatural critters. I figured by mixing iron filings with herbs, maybe even soaking the filings in certain elixirs, I could essentially create a hand held flak cannon that would deliver a lethal or banishing mixture with enough stopping power to even make Mr. Grin pause.

I smiled at the thought of turning the tables on the horrid, well-dressed ghoul. Ending him before he could ever threaten me or, more importantly, my loved ones ever again. I wasn't a killer, I wasn't *normally* a killer, I corrected my own thought. I had been forced to kill ghouls before in the interest of self-preservation. And if I had been left alone with those cultists ... who knew what would have happened. The truth was there was more blood on my hands than I cared to admit. I had served in the IDF, I had certainly been responsible for deaths during the wars I had been a part of. Again, I could always pass the blame, I could always say it was in self-preservation. But I had made the choices that had put me in a position where those choices had to be made.

I printed the spreadsheet and then saved my work. It looked more like a recipe book than anything an exorcist might use. Each column listed ingredients that would be useful against a similar array of enemies or boogeymen. If it worked. So much of what I did was experimentation. Trying to find the balance between the occult, mythology, and the cold hard truths of claw and fang. If these worked, I would owe Jon an entire series of lunches. Another thing to expense back to the Beit Din.

I closed the spreadsheet and opened my browser. Now was the less fun part. I needed to do research.

I pulled out several books, among them, Rabbi Geoffrey Dennis's *Encyclopedia of Jewish Myth* and Natan Slifkin's *Sacred Monsters*. I had more esoteric texts, but I had already pulled through those, reading everything I could. Now I was looking for other people, scholars as opposed to mystics. In Slifkin's work, I found something interesting. There were Talmudic explanations for people who could turn themselves into wolves as well as a detailed explanation why Benjamin, son of Jacob was a werewolf. Genesis 49.27 referred to Benjamin as a ravenous wolf who devours prey in the morning and divided the plunder of his work in the evening. The most rational explanation for this was allegory, of course. Benjamin made war, killing during the day and counting the spoils of his terror at night.

But Rabbi Ephraim, in his analysis of the Torah, went further, proposing that because the Torah said Benjamin dwelled between the shoulders, that was a reference to the change to wolf starting between the shoulders. He also was supposedly born with teeth and devoured his mother, who died during childbirth. Interestingly, according to Torah, Rachel had called her son Ben-Oni, which roughly means *Son of Pain,* or *Son of_Strength,* but

Jacob had gone on to call him Benjamin, *Son of the Right Hand*. Had Benjamin been a monster at birth? His life would be a hardship and his descendants blamed for so much ill. But was it possible they were more than human, that they were cursed from that moment that poor Rachel passed? And if it were true, and all of Benjamin's descendants were predatory wolves, why was this the first werewolf I was dealing with? According to Rabbi Ephraim, all I needed to do was wave a hot poker around to discourage a werewolf. But seeing as my werewolf had sat through the Bastrop fires, I figured he had come upon some way to overcome that particular fear.

I needed to find more about my specific werewolf, which meant searching for a tiny needle in the world largest electronic haystack. I typed in my best guess on spelling Peter Stübbe's name. And then tried another, and then a third. Of course, each attempt brought up hundreds of results. Results I scrolled through mindlessly, unsure what I was even looking for—arrest records maybe? I paused on my fourth attempt at spelling the name. There at the top of the search results was a Wikipedia article on a Peter Stumpp, a German serial killer who had been executed for witchcraft, cannibalism … and werewolfery.

I opened the page and read the article. It listed a dozen aliases—Stumpf, Stumpp, Stübbe, Abal Griswold—and even more crimes. The list of terrifying things that the so called werewolf of Bedford was accused of was somewhat disturbing. Fourteen children—fourteen children that they knew about—whose bodies they had found. Including his own son. According to the article, he had also had an incestuous relationship with his own daughter, herself a product of incest. I sat back in my chair staring at the woodcutting of

Stübbe getting his head cut off.

This man was executed in the 1500s. And he only had one hand; considering the Talmudic possibility of being the descendant of a guy named "Son of the Right Hand," that was a bit ironic. But the Stübbe attacking me couldn't be the same man as in this woodcutting, could it? There was, of course, the possibility that it was in fact the same person but he had used magic to survive the damage to his body—after all, I had shot the man in the face and he had shaken it off. It was also possible that it was just an alias chosen by my werewolf for some twisted sense of kinship. The question was, if he had been with his daughter, and she was also a practitioner of dark magics, was she really dead? According to the article, he had been tied to a wheel, his limbs broken with the blunt side of an axe so that he couldn't rise again from the grave, and then he was tortured, beheaded, and burned. His daughter and lover was flayed, strangled, and burned on the same pyre. I didn't know a much more comprehensive way to kill a man. If that didn't do it, what could?

I felt my stomach lurch as I read on. He had described killing pregnant woman and eating the still living fetuses as being little morsels. I needed to put an end to this monster, no matter what. If he was the original Peter Stübbe, he needed to pay for his countless crimes against humanity. If he simply styled himself after a long dead serial killer, well, it wasn't much better. I shut the laptop with a click and stood up. I didn't think some silver buckshot was going to do it. Jon's words floated into my mind. I needed to end this. End it completely. Luckily, I had something at the workshop that would do the trick, a weapon of mass destruction that was sort of the doomsday option for supernatural threats.

I smiled grimly as I walked into the bathroom

to start my shower. This was a supernatural threat worse than most I had come across. He was an immortal cannibal magician murderer, and I ... I was simply dust. But the universe was made for me, and I would end him.

Chapter 13

I spent most of the morning dealing with the small details that go into my work, filling out reports and paperwork, filing away information that would be pertinent to the Beit Din. I also finally made an official report regarding Peter Stübbe and the murder of Jewish children. This was officially my work now. This also helped in case I was killed in the line of duty: whoever they had to replace me could dive in, see my research, and at least know some of what was going on. They would also know what I had died trying and so maybe not have to get killed themselves. It was grim work.

I also made a small report on my encounters with the Sheyd that was masquerading as Officer Stevens. I wasn't sure what his game was, but you never could be sure with those sorts of creatures. While he was terrifying and menacing, I knew he wasn't working with the werewolf. It also seemed like he didn't want me dead. I wondered if he was actually after me or if his interest lay in Sandy. Which brought up a bunch of other questions. Why was Sandy attracting so much Sheydim attention? These were all puzzles I needed to figure out before it all came to a head.

First thing first, I needed to get to the office and grab my secret weapon. That and I still had some of Stübbe's hair that I had used to track him the first time. I needed to stop him before he could hurt any more children. I hopped in my car and headed towards the warehouse. While on the way there, I put some music on, letting the less than smooth voice of Tom Waits relax me while I drove. I liked weird story tellers. Tom Waits, Ray Wylie Hubbard, really if you had a voice like you ate a pack of cigarettes for breakfast and sung stories about strange things, I would probably be into it. I wondered why I was attracted to that sort of storytelling. My life was strange enough as was. I had fought vampires in Israel, trained in the use of the true alefbet by an angel, and went toe to toe with monsters and magicians. Did I really need strangeness in my media?

Maybe it was listening to things that were purely imaginative. I had to spend so much of my time parsing through people's bizarre beliefs, looking for the kernels of truth in a myriad of legends about, let's say, werewolves, that being able to just consume a story without worrying if the scary thing was actually coming for me was a little bit of a relief. That did turn my mind towards the scary things coming for me.

I knew I was a beacon for the supernatural, that I was more likely than other people to encounter things that most people didn't think existed. That was just a fact of life. I thought I understood how that worked for creatures like the dybbuk and Sheydim. My brushes with the supernatural marked me in some way that they could sense. But what about other creatures, and what about the necromancers? Why were they coming into my life? As far as I knew, magic users couldn't just sense each other as a matter of course. And what about

Stübbe, the werewolf? Was my mere presence in the community bringing danger to members of my congregation? I had never heard of anything like that, but it seemed too horrifying to just be a coincidence. But on the other hand, most of these human or semi-human threats I faced seemed to not have any clue as to who I was until I got in there and gummed up their works.

Basken discovered me because I banished an evil spirit he had been trying to unleash on the world. Stübbe didn't know I existed until I stumbled over his wards in the woods and shot him in the face. Human evil was different than supernatural creatures. It was worse, far worse. As much as I despised the ghouls who fed on corpses, they were nothing when compared against the horrid crimes of the men and women who created corpses. There was a popular debate in the Beit Din about the true nature of the Holocaust and Germany's final solution. What manner of creature had truly been pulling the strings of those events? We wanted to pinpoint the evil behind them.

But those same people never attributed other mass murderers to the supernatural. The same men who claimed that Hitler was some horrible evil Sheyd also readily attributed the evil of humans to Polpot and to African genocides. It frustrated me on a deep level. So much of the teachings in synagogue circled around being good, not just for our own community but for the worldwide community. And then so many ignored the wider issues facing the world. The hunger, the violence, the pain. I felt like, if we were going to actually engage in Tikkun Olam, the healing of the world, we couldn't be blind to the plight of gentiles. We either all healed together or we lived in the blood and mud of pain together.

With my thoughts suitably dark, I parked my car

outside the little warehouse park where Rivkah and I did our work and got out of the car. It took me a minute to gather all my things from the passenger seat, and I made a note to actually clean out the rest of my car before I took Sandy anywhere again—if she would be willing to go anywhere with me after our encounter. I sighed and walked towards the door of our workshop …

And froze.

The door hung open. I could see blood.

✡

The blood was streaked across the door frame, and there were streaks of blood on the ground. The worst thing, it appeared to be hours old. My heart sank from my chest into my stomach. I ran back to the car to grab my Jericho 941 before running back to the warehouse and kicking the loose door wide. I swung the gun around, covering the corners and blind spots. My warehouse, my safe haven, was torn apart. It had been tossed, and there was debris everywhere. Books flung across the room haphazardly, papers, craft supplies, metals, scientific equipment, even furniture had all been thrown around in an attempt to destroy everything. But it was Rivkah, who lay in a broken heap in the center of it all, that arrested my attention. I holstered my gun and ran to her.

It was bad. Her face and arms were covered in bruises, one of her eyes swollen shut. There were bite marks in her legs; she looked like they had been toying with her. I didn't want to call the hospital; I didn't want to check her pulse. Because if I checked her pulse and it wasn't there, I really think it would have killed me. I was still struggling with my own fear when she let out a ragged moan.

My heart soared for a second. She was alive but unconscious. I immediately got on the phone, dialing 911. After a second, they answered.

"Nine-one-one, what is your emergency?" The voice on the other end of the phone was calm, assured.

"My friend has been attacked. She's hurt very bad. Please send an ambulance!" I nearly shouted the address to her before she could ask. I heard typing on the other end.

"Okay, sir, is she breathing?"

"Yes."

"Is she conscious?"

"No."

"Okay, how did this happen, sir? Is there any danger to others?"

"I don't think so, I don't see ..." I paused, seeing a note, a scrawled note sitting on my otherwise empty desk. It looked like it had been finger-painted in blood. Rivkah's blood. My hand tightened on my phone.

"Sir?" the voice asked to my sudden silence.

I didn't answer, though. The note had my full attention.

Tired of playing games.
Waiting outside Dell City, Julie's Diner.
Sandy is nice, taking an inch of skin
For every hour I wait.
-P

I hung up. Dell City was far. I had only driven through it once, but it was clear on the other side of Texas, nearer El Paso than anything, a good 450 miles. And I didn't know how much of a head start the motherfucker had on me. I looked back at Rivkah. There wasn't much I could do for her; the ambulance would be coming. I needed to get to Sandy, I needed to stop this monster. I moved back to Rivkah's side, stroking her cheek with the back of my fingers. This was because of me, because I couldn't not get involved.

Now I had to get to the other side of the damn state as quickly as possible. Sandy would die if I dragged my feet, if she was even still alive. I couldn't let this happen; I couldn't allow him to hurt her. She was my responsibility, and he only went after her because I had been stupid enough to expose her. My brain ached as I tried to figure out how to make things right, as I wondered if things even could be made right. I had no options. I had to leave Rivkah here and start driving immediately; even then, how late would I be? Unless ...

My eyes slid over to the safe where I kept the proscribed texts. Magic that warped reality. That could warp time and space. A trip of 400 miles would be nothing to the Sheydim. I had a solution. A forbidden, terrible solution. What was worth more, my rules, the rules of the Beit Din, or the life of Sandy Cohen? It wasn't even a question. I gave Rivkah's hand a squeeze, then rose and moved to open the safe.

Inside were all the books I had gathered over the long years of doing this. I had come across some of them organically, seen them in collections or stumbled on them in the hands of monsters. I took them and hid them away so no one could use them. The majority, however, I had gathered at the behest of Grin. I never planned to give them to him, but I had found them and hoarded them. Now ... now I was going to use one of the books, one in particular.

I put in the code and threw open the safe, scanning the contents quickly. These were terrible texts, but in them was the power to protect Sandy. I grabbed Dhol Chants, a damned book said to be written in the language of a pre-human race. That could mean anything; it could just be a bunch of bullshit, but I was hoping it meant the Sheydim. I opened it, scanning the pages. I had opened it once before to confirm what it was, to see what was in it. That was all I allowed myself with any of these texts.

But now I was searching each page, looking through the strange words in an unfamiliar language. It seemed to be a bastardization of ancient Hebrew and German in a Greek alphabet. Having spent most of my life studying religion, knowing both modern and ancient Hebrew as well as being conversational in Yiddish helped me out, but I still stumbled. I was looking for a key word. After several minutes of searching, I found what I was looking for. A chant and ritual for 'safe passage'. I hoped it meant teleportation and not just a blasphemous prayer towards keeping safe while traveling. I scanned the ritual for a few moments. I had everything I needed.

I set the book on a lectern that I dragged over to a clear space on the floor and then moved to the shelves to gather everything I needed. Crematory ashes, bones from a black rooster, and chalk. The ritual called for the chalk to be dipped in blood before being used to draw the damned sigils; luckily, there was no shortage of spilled sticky blood on the floor. I worked as fast as I could while still maintaining focus. In magic, intention and kavanagh are the single most important ingredients. It was difficult to maintain the focus while Rivkah lay injured so close to me. But medical help was on its way, and I needed to have finished the ritual and gone to West Texas before they got here.

Finishing the set up, I stood at the lectern and began reading the scrawling chant as best I could. In theory, the Greek alphabet was phonetic, but as with Hebrew, it was the vowels and combination letters that could ruin your pronunciation, and I didn't have much cause to read Greek these days. But I pushed on, worried that when the medical staff got here, I would still be standing before an evil looking circle I drew in my assistant's blood while she lay horribly injured just feet away. I was through my fifth recitation of the chant when someone behind me cleared their throat. I spun around as a shadow detached itself from the wall and strode towards me, solidifying into a tall, terrifying man with glowing red eyes. When he spoke, it was in a voice that had the weight of time, the gravitas of power. It was deep and reverberated in the room and in my skull. It gestured towards the summoning diagram I had drawn.

"I'll pass on the circle."

✡

The man was jet black, black as the night, and wore black robes that shimmered as though they contained the stars. Despite being cut from the infinite void, red eyes, and being taller than goliath, he looked remarkably human. There was something insubstantial about him, but at the same time, he had a presence that I had only felt when face to face with Domah. This being was ancient, powerful, and he was here, unconstrained by the laws of magic, because of me.

He must have processed my shocked face because he asked, "Did you not expect your little chant to work? Did you expect for your friend here to die? I assume that is why you called me? To save her?" He kept walking towards me. I thought he might just approach me and kill me where I stood, but he stopped just a few feet away. His eyes glittered, they were less diabolic and more like rubies set in an obsidian statue.

"I, no, I have a medical team coming to save her. I need passage." I finally managed to answer the creature. What was he? Sheydim? He was nothing like the other Sheydim I had met. This man, this shard of shadow was monstrously powerful, it came off him like a sickening, threatening aura.

"Passage? Do I look like a cabbie to you? Do you know what you were chanting? What you risk? For passage! I am disappointed, Ze'ev; you of all people should know better than to abuse power." He spoke almost off-handedly, but he sounded more amused than annoyed.

I was getting frustrated by all of these supernatural threats knowing my name like it was nothing. He wasn't even looking at me; instead, his eyes moved over the warehouse, taking in the destruction and the calamity of my life.

"My apprentice, a young girl, was taken, by a ruthless killer. They've gone to the other side of the state, and I need to catch them, I need to save *her*." I didn't know why I was explaining the whys of the situation to the Sheyd. He was here for a deal, he wouldn't care about the story. "Can you help me get there in time to save her?"

"I can," he said before looking back at me.

I pressed on. "Save her alive, intact, before he takes away her ability to have a quality life, and get me there in one piece with my—"

He interrupted me by raising a six-fingered hand. "I am not a faerie, Ze'ev. Whatever compact we reach, I honor the spirit of it, not just the word. And I expect the same from you, agreements made in good faith. Yes, I can get you there whole to save the child whole. But not for nothing, balance must be kept, so ..." He paused, his eyes narrowing as they watched me. "A life for a life. Who to you is worth less than your apprentice? Who will die in her place?"

This at least I could answer with no hesitation. "I will. My life for hers."

"No." He said it lazily, with no malice or attempt

to hide his amusement.

"No?" I stumbled over the word. I had been pretty sure that would work, it always worked in ... movies. It always worked in stupid ass movies, and I had made the most amateur mistake of conflating reality with media.

"No," he repeated. "Your type always think that is the answer. You think you get to poison your soul using dark magics and then clean the slate with a selfless sacrifice. No, a sacrifice isn't about getting what you want, it's about giving something up. It's about giving up a piece of yourself. So no, you do not get to sacrifice yourself in some stupid fucking gesture, Ze'ev. Another life, another death. Perhaps ..." He turned his head and looked at Rivkah.

"Don't you fucking look at her!" I roared. I grabbed his chin and wrenched his face back towards me. Or I tried. It was like trying to force a statue to change its pose.

He looked at me. His eye sockets slid in his skull until they faced me, narrowed in silent rage before the rest of his face turned and the sockets stayed in place, reassembling his visage. He looked down at my hand in warning. I let go, properly terrified.

"No, not her. Then who? Tick-tock, Ze'ev," he said, crossing his arms over his chest.

My mind spun out of control. Who could I condemn in place of Sandy? The easy answer was Basken or one of his little goons, G-d knows I wanted to kill them the other day when they attacked me here, for what they did to Kristine. But they were all in prison, that cost me nothing. I said it, they died, and the world was a little better off. This monster in front of me wanted me to damn myself to save Sandy. Fine. I would play his game.

"Peter Stübbe," I answered finally. "The werewolf of Bedford. His life."

The Sheydim rocked back on his heels,

considering my offer. "You were going to kill him anyway," he finally answered me.

"Yes, but I'll do it in your name, or whatever. It's not selfless, it's selfish. I want to kill him. That's what you want, right? You want me to poison myself?"

"No, I want you to do what is necessary, I want you to prove yourself." He tapped his chin. "You are saying that the life of a young innocent girl is worth more than a near immortal child murdering cannibal rapist? How transgressive."

"Do we have a deal or not?" I asked, shoving my hand forward like an 80s business man trying to close a terrible trade.

"We have a deal," he responded, enveloping my hand in his own. His six-fingered grip was warm and surprisingly human. "Gather your weapons, gather what you'll need to make good on your agreement and rescue the girl while I open your way."

I was terrified of turning my back on the Sheyd, but I did what he asked. I grabbed charms and amulets for my own protection. My Jericho was still in my holster, but I added knuckle dusters inscribed with angelic blessings and my butterfly knife. Neither would make a permanent dent in Stübbe, but I also had my secret weapon. I grabbed it and shoved it into a long thin canvas carrying case I had ordered for it. When I came back to the Sheyd's side, he stood next to a pulsing rend in reality.

"You will travel through the City East of Nod, the bastion and home of the Sheydim. You will not be safe there, but you will run straight down the street I have set you on, and you will reach a portal like this one. Go through it, and you will arrive at your apprentice's side in time to save her." The Sheydim took my chin in his hand and forced me to look up into his eyes, a mirror of my own attempt to do so earlier, only far more successful. "You will not take out your weapons, you unleash none of this." He gestured to the bag I was carrying. "If you should use a weapon in the City East of Nod, I will know, and I will rip you, your apprentice, and that woman apart myself. Stübbe will be a kindness compared to my rage. This is part of our agreement. Do you understand?"

I swallowed but nodded. I was going to travel through an entire realm of Sheydim with no protection, but I just had to make my way down one street. How terrible could it be?

"I understand the terms," I finally answered.

He released me.

"Go now; and, Ze'ev?"

I paused at the edge of the hole in space and looked back at him.

"Good luck." He smiled, and it was the strangest, kindest smile I had seen on a supernatural being's face in all my years. I wanted to comment, I wanted to figure it out, but with those final words, he put a six-fingered hand on my chest and shoved me through the hole in space.

Chapter 14

I felt like I was being ripped apart. Like there were a thousand of me all kaleidoscoping through a passage of infinite colors. Colors that burned my mind. My body was contorted and abused, twisted and changed, a mercurial reality in which I was like latke mix being kneaded by the universe. If I still had a stomach—and let me be frank, I didn't know if I did—it would have been twisted and churned and vomited out anything I had ever eaten across all of time. All around me, stars and strange alien beings moved, shuffling closer to me, drawn to my all too human mortal soul. I screamed from one of the millions of mouths that made up my being in that moment. And then I had one mouth. I was still screaming, but I was screaming while kneeling on a road made of cobblestone.

I stopped screaming and sat there, on my knees in the middle of the street, panting. My mind was still a fractured thing, and slowly, my thoughts and consciousness came back to me, like pieces of a puzzle falling together. I felt like I had been a game of Tetris, with bits and parts of me sliding into place, leaving gaps in who I was just big enough for there to be doubts.

After several minutes of just existing, I looked around … and I wished I hadn't.

I was in the middle of a massive stone city. It reminded me of New York. Buildings stretched up around me, reaching for … for a cavernous ceiling far above. The entire city was underground. Stalactites that had to be the size of skyscrapers hung above us, and I could see distant lights, luminescent mold and fungi provided a star like quality to the distant stone sky. This was the City East of Nod. Nod was east of Eden, according to the Torah, where Cain had been banished after slaying Abel. But from the name, this was farther than Nod, this was into the wilderness where Talmudic lore said demons originated. I was guessing; however, this wasn't a place that one could find in the physical world. It was separate.

I had heard of the City East of Nod before. In my dealings with some of the Sheydim, in obscure texts, in places where most people didn't look. It was also a passing mention, never anything solid. And I had to admit, I had envisioned something a bit more ren-fair than modern metropolis. But that was what I was seeing here. Though I didn't see much metal, everything was built of stone and precious gems, there were streetlights, lights on in the buildings. Something rode past me on a bicycle, waving its fist and cursing at me in a language I didn't understand.

There were food trucks. I saw a hot dog cart.

That made me laugh out loud. For all my preconceived notions, for the mystery and mysticism and mythology built around these creatures, they lived in a city like anyone else. But the denizens … I spent a moment to look around me, at the other beings on the street I was on. They came in all colors and sizes. I saw Satyr, bat winged creatures, things that I had fought, and things I had run from. Creatures from almost every legend I had ever read or heard about populated the street. Off to the side, I saw what looked like a centaur buying a falafel wrap.

Something happens when a young human encounters a supernatural force. It marks them, it makes them more visible to the supernatural. To the Sheydim. As I slowly pulled myself up from the ground, the beings around me began to take notice. As I caught their eyes, I arrested their attention. I was aware that within moments, every eye of every creature on that street was turned towards me. I felt the weight of the gun in my shoulder holsters. It was weighed down by the threats the Sheyd back in my warehouse had made. But would those threats matter if I was torn apart? I started walking, hoping that keeping calm and acting like I was exactly where I should be would protect me from being attacked. Running, I assumed, would just trigger their predator instinct.

But I did walk briskly. I tried to keep my eyes straight ahead, on my goal, but I felt like a country bumpkin on my first trip to a big city. I suppose it wasn't that inaccurate a description. I had been to big cities, but I had never been to a city as breathtaking as the City East of Nod. Try as I might, I couldn't shake the overwhelming knowledge that I was one of a very small number of living humans who had set foot in this city. Not only that, I was an exorcist and hunter. I had made my life battling against supernatural forces that threatened the Jewish people. How many of the denizens in this place had I pissed off? I ducked my head and hurried.

From what little I could tell, though, I wasn't being chased, I wasn't being followed. Other than the eyes of beings I was passing by. I needed to get off the main street. While the Sheyd I had summoned had told me it was a straight shot, I just needed to not be so visible. I ducked down a side alley on my right, and was relieved to be alone. If this city truly was like New York, it would be built on a grid, I would be able to turn left, and follow the next street for a while, work the back alleyways until I found the rift in space that the summoned Sheyd had been talking about.

The City East of Nod was an uncanny valley. So much like the world I knew, but different in important and mind-bending ways. First, there was no litter, no garbage on the streets. No homeless that I could see. The entities I did see walked around in a strange mix of clothing from all ages. I saw bat-like men in tunics and a woman wearing something that looked like it was ripped off from a cyberpunk porno magazine. Everywhere I looked, the clash of culture and style was almost jarring. It was a true melting pot as monsters from all over the world and from all time periods lived together in what I could only assume was a kind of harmony. I wished I could stay, I wished I could catalog the strange sights that so few could see. But in the back of my head, pushing me ever forward, was my mission to save Sandy and the knowledge that no matter how interesting this place was, it was also deadly.

I exited an alley back onto the main street and was surprised by the lack of other people on this stretch of the street. It was practically empty, which suited me just fine. But my experience so far had been that this city didn't sleep, didn't rest. As I started forward again, shapes began emerging from behind garbage cans and from within doorways. I understood why this section had been empty, it was a trap. I took a step back, maybe I could flee back down the ally, but then I saw more shapes emerging to block my exit.

As they entered the light given off by the streetlamps, my heart sank. I recognized Baladan. A curious mixture of baboon, bat, and dog, Baladan was a messenger of sorts for the Sheydim. The last time I had seen him, he had alerted nightmares to my presence in the world of dreams. He cackled as he loped forward on knuckles that were too large for his slight frame. The other things in the shadows revealed themselves to be of the same species as Baladan. One of them was massive, like a silverback gorilla with the face of a coyote and great leathery wings that drooped from his folded arms. I looked around wildly, unsure how I could escape this ambush without using any weapons.

"Sorcerer, little wolf, big bad Ze'ev." Baladan cackled his greeting from between broken jagged teeth. "I warned you, I warned you, do not involve yourself in the courts of the Sheydim, do not, do not, do not." All of this was mumbled in sing song malice as the creature danced in front of me. "This is not, not meddling, little wolf, this is not, not being involved. You are so involved, you are in our city, our home." His smile dropped and he screamed at me. "You should not be here! You will not leave here!"

The creatures advanced on me. I looked around wildly, seeking some avenue of escape. There was none. The deal-making Sheyd hadn't said I couldn't fight, only that I couldn't use any weapons. Fine. I gritted my teeth and glared at Baladan. "Fuck you."

I launched myself at the little Sheyd. He was small, but he was quick. He leapt up and onto my shoulder before jumping again and pushing me down. I whirled, trying to get him back in sight, but there were so many of the little things that I was having trouble figuring out which of the imps was him. They also weren't going to let me whale on one of them. They came all at once, biting, scratching, punching. I dodged where I could, tearing the smaller Sheydim off of me and tossing them aside while I rolled under the gangly arms of an orangutan/wolf hybrid thing. All in all, I was doing no damage to them. I was already covered in scratches and little bites. But I thought maybe I could get free and make a break for it. All I had to do was get past them and outpace them. Easy ...

I dodged under Baladan as he leapt at me and pushed through to get clear of them, when the massive creature that resembled a gorilla grabbed me by the shoulder. He lifted me with no strain and slammed me back into the ground. The world shook, and my vision swam, the entire City East of Nod blurred. I wondered if I had a concussion. And then it lifted me back into the air and threw me. I soared through the air, tumbling end over end, before I crashed into a wall. I felt something inside me pop. Something was broken, but I couldn't focus on that. I pulled myself away from the wall and looked at the cackling Sheydim approaching me. I couldn't win this fight. I would die here and now unless I did something drastic.

I raised my arms and intoned the true pronunciation of the letter *Mem*. Power washed out from me. The street trembled as I exerted my will over reality even here in this place detached from my own world. I stepped forward pronouncing the next sound. If spelled out, it would be a *vav*, but this was a vowel. An eh sound in the human language, but a secret and true sound that cracked stone as it pushed from my mouth and roared down the street, pushing the Sheydim back like the wind of a tornado. Spelling a full word in the true language of creation, especially a word of destruction, was dangerous. To me, human bodies weren't meant to wield that kind of power. Baladan realized what

I was spelling. His eyes wide with fear, he turned to run, they all turned to flee me. It was too late. I opened my mouth to pronounce the *Tav*, the final letter in the word Death.

Tav ripped from my body and was birthed into the world like the fury of a hurricane, rushing forward on the wings of willpower across the street. Where it was met by the true pronunciation of the silent letter *Aleph*. The silent letter dashed my own proclamation apart, pushed past it, and hit me. I was lifted into the air, and I felt every bone in my body shatter into dust, my organs burst in their flimsy sacks, and then it all froze. In that moment of agony and death. A single nanosecond more and I would be dead. I was already dead, it was just a matter of letting it happen.

She stepped past the sheydim, who cowered and whimpered in her presence. She was the single most beautiful thing I had ever seen. My eyes couldn't look away from her, my mind refused to think of anything other than her. She was everything. The woman approaching me looked like a goddess of sex and fertility. Of lust and motherhood. Nude and perfect. She was every characterization of sensuality all smashed into one. From her feet that seemed to walk above the earth to her long, dreaded hair, I couldn't spot a single blemish or imperfection on her ebony skin. Her stomach was taut, but with the fullness of a woman who had born children. Her breasts were heavy and round, begging to be held, touched, kissed. Her eyes, the whites glowing in such dark skin, met mine. And I almost moaned my longing at her. Her body was lithe and strong, but curved and welcoming. Offering all the strength of a warrior queen and all the softness of a concubine. Her full dark lips curled back from sparkling white teeth in what looked like a snarl, but my lusting needful mind translated as an alluring smile. I needed her. I needed her to love me, to want me, as I loved, wanted, and needed her.

She walked through the demons towards me. Whenever I spoke the silent Aleph, it was a jolt, a sudden reality shaping moment that passed and crashed back in on itself. To hold it in place for even a moment, let alone this long as she was doing, was an act of monstrous, almost inconceivable will power. She stopped in front of me, tall and imperious. I felt my broken body, a collection of powdered bones and ruptures organs, long to react. If my heart hadn't already exploded in my chest, it would have been pumping blood through my body to welcome her.

"So, it's you." Her words were in a language I couldn't understand, but my mind supped in the exotic language that sounded like caramel drizzled across the body before being licked up and translated them. I couldn't respond, my tongue had been shredded by the shrapnel of my teeth as they broke. Only my mind and thoughts seemed to be working. And each of those thoughts was about my need for this woman, this goddess.

"Why you, son of Jacob?" She stepped closer, and I could feel her body press into my skin. I couldn't even feel agony as her nipples pressed into me, my lust was overpowering every other sensation that existed.

She stepped back and placed a hand against my face. It was soft and warm and inviting. I wanted to close my eyes and disappear in that sensation. "Why have you arrested his attention?" She leaned forward and put her forehead against mine. I would have thought it would be less painfully alluring than when her whole body was pressed into me. I was would have been wrong. "Why?" she repeated, and I felt her inside my brain. This didn't break the spell entirely, her intrusion felt intimate, loving. But it was still an intrusion.

I could feel her sifting through my thoughts and memories. She was taking over my mind. Something in me rebelled. I tried to fill my mind with other thoughts, to block my complete lustful surrender. I blocked her mind slithering through my mind by thinking of the woman I betrayed with my need for this goddess. I thought of my mother, Ruth, and my sisters. But I felt her mind wrap around the image and push it aside.

"Do not worry about your mother, your mother is precious to me, all mothers are ..." she cooed, and I felt my body want to spasm at the sound of her voice.

I thought of Rivkah, who lay bleeding in my warehouse. I had left her in the company of that one Sheyd! My mind reeled away from the goddess as I tried to remember if I had worked Rivkah's safety into our deal. The succubus, she had to be succubus, pulled my mind back to her, and I sank into her mind's embrace.

"No, not her, a good woman, better than you deserve to know, I think ..." She guided me away from Rivkah, so easily pulling me away from my panic.

I wanted to rebel, but her hold on me was absolute.

I thought of Sandy ... but that soon fell away as the succubus ignored it without even a moment's hesitation.

"No, do not worry, time is different here, we can take as much of it as we need, and I will not make you late ..." The teased promise of taking our time lingered on her perfect lips.

Despairingly, as my body ached for the inhuman creature before me, I thought about Sara, who I was betraying merely though my want. If I was not frozen, if I was not about to die, I wouldn't have hesitated to take this woman in my arms and love her right there in the street. I couldn't fight it. I couldn't go against the need that screamed through my body. But as I thought of Sara's face and our rocky relationship, the succubus reeled back from me. The sudden withdrawal from my mind would have elicited a painful moan, perhaps a scream, if my mouth or lungs were working. The sudden absence of such an intimate interaction made me feel cold and alone and more full of a need for this woman than I had ever needed anything before that moment.

She stared at me in silence for what felt like several minutes. The world froze, and it was just us. Her in mute judgment, me in a lustful agony beyond any description.

She whispered a silent sound, and the world crashed back to what it was. My bones came together, cracks and fissures sealing and healing. My organs reformed, and time reversed from that moment of her first silent Aleph. I fell to the ground and caught myself, breathing hard. I looked up at her, and was in awe of the goddess of sex and comfort in front of me. Her pure power and perfection called to my every cell. I rose and stepped towards her. I needed the intimacy again, I would surrender everything for it.

She slapped me. My head snapped to the side, my entire world shaken. I had the realization that this creature had only used a fraction of her incredible strength to slap me, but still my vision was blurred and I saw stars. When I looked forward again, she was wearing robes of cyan and gold that had not been there before. Even covered as she was, I still ached for her. But now my mind was cleared, I could control myself. She had used the slap to clear my mind. I touched my cheek where a bruise was already forming.

"Thank you," I whispered, so grateful to be freed and so terrified of this woman, I could think of nothing else to say.

She regarded me without menace; in her eyes was only a sort of sad affection.

"You have struck a deal with an important man to me. I honor his deal; go. Go with my protection and save the girl." She stepped aside.

I almost argued. I wanted to stay, to worship at her feet. Such a blasphemy, I was dumbfounded by my own idiocy. I gritted my teeth and nodded, turning away from her and running before I could have a second, or fourth, thought of serving such a creature. As I ran, I glanced over my shoulder and saw Baladan's posse of horrible baboon demons crawling back into the shadows and the woman, the succubus, watching me. She raised a hand, and I thought she was going to wave at me, but then a shadow rose behind her like a tsunami and crashed down over the street at my back. The darkness began to coalesce into a monstrous draconic shape. I didn't want to see what that was. I fled as fast as my feet would carry me. She had told me to save Sandy; she had looked at my entire life and found me worthy of living. I could take some succor in that, but I didn't want to push my luck.

✡

After a block, life returned to normal, away from Baladan's ambush. The Sheydim watched me, a mortal, running full tilt through their city, but not a one sought to detain or stop me. They took one look at me, looked back towards whatever was behind me, and then pointedly minded their own damn business. I didn't know what was behind me, I didn't want to know. The shape that had begun to take form in the darkness the succubus was summoning had been terrifying. My lungs were burning from the constant exertion. Ahead, I saw the rip in time that the Sheyd had talked about. I thought about diving through the portal, escaping this world as quickly as possible. But doing so would put me on the other side, among the enemy, exhausted and out of breath. I slowed my flight and finally stumbled to a stop just beside the portal and bent over, gasping for breath, trying to recover some measure of stamina.

I heard the steps of someone approaching, and I closed my mind, cursing my terrible luck. Couldn't the Sheydim give me a break? Couldn't I have one moment to breathe before I had to die at the hands of some terrible descendant of a biblical figure? I didn't stand up straight or open my eyes as the steps came closer and finally stopped next to me.

"What?" I asked, trying to sound tough and casual all at once, like I was supposed to be here.

"Don't be rude. You are in my home, my city, you are the one who does not belong." The voice was powerful but had enough gravel in it to be classified as a growl, like some sort of uber-Tom Waits. To be honest, I was just relieved it wasn't the succubus. I didn't think I could resist her.

I finally looked up.

The man was olive skinned, bald, and powerfully built. He wore a black suit that looked to be made of alligator skin, though I couldn't be sure it wasn't his actual skin. The air blurred around him making definitive details difficult. His orange eyes were slit like a serpent's, and he regarded me with a sort of dismissive boredom that would have been offensive anywhere but here.

"Okay ..." I finally responded. "Sorry, it's been a bad day." I remembered what the succubus said; time moved different here, I wouldn't be late, I wouldn't be killing Sandy by taking time to recover. "I'm about to leave, though, I promise." I took a deep breath and stood up straight, trying to look heroic in a way that was completely not me.

"I know, Queen Lilit bat HaShem bid me see you here safely." His orange eyes, glowing ever so slightly, turned away from me, and he looked over the city. "It's been quite a while since a mortal human has been here, you should feel honored, even more honored that the Queen took an interest in your existence."

"Li ... That was Lillith?" I hissed the name in a harsh whisper. Lillith, the queen of demons and Sheydim, Adam's first wife, the very first woman, mother of all succubi. I could feel my stomach drop. Being noticed by creatures as old and powerful as the Sheydim was terrifying enough by itself without adding things like demigods to the mix.

"Yes." The olive skinned man nodded, then gestured at the portal. "Time to go. Even with my protection, the citizens of our city will be curious. They will come, they will follow. It is best for both of us, I believe, that we avoid that."

I stared into the orange eyes, trying to put into words how overwhelmed I was, but I realized it didn't matter. It didn't matter that I had fallen in love and lust with the first woman to ever exist. It didn't matter that I had gotten into a fist fight with a gang of baboon demons. All that mattered was that I had made it to the end of the street, to the portal that would lead me to Sandy. I patted my pockets, checking. Gun, check. Knife, check. I still had my amulets, my knuckle dusters, and of course, my canvas bag. It was time to go. I nodded a simple thanks to the olive skinned Sheyd and plunged through the rip in space.

The second time was easier than the first. Yes, I still felt like everything was being unmade and stretched apart. As though my soul was leaking through my eyes in multi-colored tears of joy and pain. But my purpose, protecting Sandy, solidified my mind and steeled me against the onslaught of physical and spiritual changes that pushing through the portal caused. My eyes, if they still existed in that moment between worlds, were set hard and focused on an end goal. I had made a deal with the proverbial devil. Faced the first woman and survived. I had punched my way through a posse of Sheydim and traveled to other realms to do this. I would not falter at this moment. I was remade in my own world a moment later. Around me, a small deserted stretch of highway town sat in the scorching early afternoon sun. It felt like a modern retelling of an old western, the broken-down diner Julie's was our saloon. But instead of two gunmen, it was just me.

Just me, surrounded by a half a dozen slathering ghouls.

Chapter 15

I looked around the group of monsters. I don't think I had ever seen the creatures in daylight. It was clear they were uncomfortable, pallid skin turning pink in the bright Texas sun. I turned in a slow circle. There were six of them, each snarling through misshapen hyena-like jaws, thick strands of drool dripping from between the yellowed shards of teeth. Their eyes, dark and sunken, were narrowed, adapted for the dark and navigating tunnels underneath cemeteries. In the bright light of day, I could see the sparse hair that bristled their skin and the sorry state of the rags they wore as clothes. They looked like the desiccated corpses their kind fed on.

But why were ghouls here? Why were these creatures in the sun?

I turned in a tight circle, and spotted Stübbe. He was leaning against the wall of an abandoned diner. The Sheyd had gotten me here after all. He smiled a terrible, cruel smile when he saw me. There was blood plastering his beard to his face in a sticky mess. I wondered if it was Rivkah's or Sandy's. I took a step forward, but so did the circle of ghouls. They were tense, just waiting to pounce and tear me apart.

"She said you would be coming through the hidden pathways," Stübbe said from his post.

"Where's the girl?" I asked, ignoring the ghouls for the moment—well, sort of ignoring them. I reached into my pocket and felt the reassuring weight of my knife.

"She's inside. You got here fast, faster than I was hoping. I haven't gotten to tear much of her skin yet," he said lazily. "I figure I can finish once we deal with you, really take my time with her, repay you for Sasha's death."

"Sasha? Was that your wolf? Your wolf that the Sheyd killed when you attacked us?" I shook my head, reached into my coat, and pulled out the Jericho. I could see the ghouls were seconds away from tearing into me. I couldn't let them kill me; I had to save Sandy and I owed the Sheydim a life. Stübbe's life. "It doesn't matter, you won't touch Sandy again."

"Oh, I doubt that. I think I'll go touch her now," he said with a full throated chuckle. "She's a little older than I prefer, but she'll still taste sweet." He pushed himself off the doorway to the warehouse and waved his hand dismissively as he went inside.

The ghouls closed on me. But I was already moving.

Ghouls are dangerous creatures, intelligent, cunning, fast, and strong. But at the core, they were untrained and sloppy scavengers. And I had been considering fighting them and training to survive this sort of engagement since my tangle with Mr. Grin and the ghoul king Baalrachius. I also didn't give a fuck at the moment. Later, I would have to grapple with the idea of killing intelligent beings. For now, these creatures were standing between me and saving a young Jewish girl from being tortured to death by a cannibal. As they came forward, my gun came up and roared.

The ghoul immediately in front of me screamed with a shattered collarbone and a hole in its throat. I lowered my head and slammed into the injured creature, bowling it over and stumbling as I broke out of the circle of death they had ringed me in and twisted. Now there were five ghouls in front of me. I fired again, the shot going wild as I was still turning. I fired again and again, my fear and rage powering my inability to think and aim clearly. Despite my haphazard shooting, a second ghoul stopped, the back of its skull exploding in a shrapnel rain. But by then, the rest had reached me. One grabbed my gun arm and pushed my hand up, and another tackled me in the middle, scrabbling at my chest with claws that drew beads of blood as it tried to get at my flesh. I dropped the gun, letting it clatter to the street.

The best part of shooting a gun is that the people you shoot at tended to hyper-focus on the firearm. The ghouls, animals that they were, hadn't even taken notice of the blade in my hand until I cut forward, slicing through the papery dry throat of the ghoul on top of me. I brought up my legs and kicked the still twitching corpse away from me as I flipped the blade around and buried it in the chest of the monster holding my arm. It squealed in surprise and tried to get a grip on the knife handle now coated in its own slippery blood. I leaned back and rocketed forward, slamming my forehead into the creature's snout. I was very satisfied by the crunch of bone and give of its muzzle. It fell back dazed.

I was about to follow it and get my knife back when I felt another hand grab my shoulder and fling me back. I landed on my side and rolled back to my feet. The two uninjured ghouls were racing for me.

I reached into my coat pockets with both hands, my left came back out, and I cried "<u>Nachash!</u>" slipping just enough of the true pronunciation and intention into the word to activate the amulet I had flung. The chain, bearing a charm carved with the image of a javelin sand boa, hit the ghoul on the right and immediately began wrapping around the creature, biting into creature, constricting and crushing it.

I didn't have time to watch the charm working, the other ghoul was on me already. My right hand came out of my coat, fingers wrapped in the knuckle dusters that had been secreted there. The names of various angels were inscribed on the metal of the brass knuckles, but I didn't invoke anything. The metal of the knuckles was plenty discouragement as I met the ghoul's charge with my own uppercut. I wish I couldn't say it was satisfying when the bone gave away under. I followed the creature as it tumbled in the street and straddled it, landing several punches to its head until it stopped moving. I didn't know if it was dead or dying, but I did know it wouldn't get up and attack me again. I stood and looked around. Two ghouls were still moving.

One writhed on the ground, fingers digging bloody ragged holes in its own throat as it tried to remove the charm. It would suffocate in a few moments. The other was sitting with its back against a wall, gurgling through broken teeth as it held its hand over the knife wound. I walked past the choking ghoul and picked my gun off the street. I watched the two dying things for a moment before moving back to the one I had snared. I touched the chain with two fingers and broke the spell. The ghoul crawled away from me, gasping for breath as it fled.

"Take your friend ... run. If I see either of you

again ..." I let the threat lie there; I didn't think I needed to explain further. I turned my back on them and walked into the diner. They had delayed me too long already. It was time to end this.

✡

The diner was in disrepair; chairs and tables had been tossed haphazardly into corners and shoved against the walls. The booths were torn up and the seats hollowed out. Broken glass and shards of plates littered the floor around me. The place looked like it had been ransacked years ago and left to rot in its own mold and dust. The hollowed-out shell of the American dream. I could see through the window to the kitchen that there was movement back there. And a flickering light. I wondered if the power actually worked or if the *shtik drek* had set up a generator to try to be more intimidating.

I heard him speaking from the back. A low growl that reverberated through the diner. He may have been whispering, but the rumble of his voice carried too easily in the stillness of that moment. He was speaking in Yiddish, more signs that the sub-human *putz* was German, that he was actually Stübbe, the werewolf of Bedford. I pushed through the swinging back door into the kitchen and saw them.

Sandy was tied to a chair with leather straps, hair matted to her face in dried blood, bruises covering her. But she was awake, and she was breathing. But a leather gag was in her mouth keeping her from calling out for help. I looked her over from across the room. I couldn't see any signs of more extreme torture, and her clothes, thank HaShem, were whole and on her. I turned from her and looked at the man standing next to her.

"Ah, he made it further than I thought he would," Peter whispered. "But that ends now, it ends now and I kill you and then I kill the girl, and then maybe I go back to Austin and kill some more. You've been too big a pain in the ass."

"Why? Why do you do this? Why are you hurting her?" I raised a hand, the one not holding the gun, and gestured at Sandy. "Just, let her go. I'm here. I'm here like you wanted me to be here."

"Oh no, she was quite clear on it; I kill you, I kill everyone you care about, and then she shows me where they buried Beele, my darling Beele. Think about that. You and your bloodline die, and in exchange, I get to bring mine back." He caressed the side of Sandy's face. Sandy recoiled in fear and disgust. "You know, she kind of reminds me of my Beele, my daughter, close to the same age. Maybe we can play some of the same games me and Beele played before I devour you, eat you all up." He snapped his teeth, then threw his head back and laughed.

That was all the invitation I needed.

I charged forward, firing twice before I heard the click of an empty magazine. I dropped the gun and leapt at him knife first. Fuck he was fast. He grabbed my arm and turned, flipping me over his shoulder and sending me flying against a far wall where several pots and pans hung. The knife clattered to the floor, and I growled, pushing myself up and trying to shield my head from falling cookware. But even as I stood, Peter was grabbing my arm, slamming me against the wall. Drywall gave beneath me, the diner shook. He landed a punch into my side and then flung me again, back towards the front of the diner. I crashed through the doors, which splintered as I hit them. I tried to catch my breath and steady myself, but Peter was there again. He wrapped one massive hand around my throat and squeezed. I couldn't breathe. I scratched at his hand as he lifted me off the ground and laughed in my face. His breath smelled of blood and death. He threw me again, this time sending me through the diner windows and onto the street.

The bodies of the ghouls were gone, cleared away by their own in an attempt to hide their presence from the human world. I scrambled to my feet to try to get into some kind of defensive posture before he hit me again, but he was taking his time, kicking debris out of his way, smiling like a maniac. I reached over my back an unzipped the long, skinny canvas bag.

"Why do you even bother? Why, Ze'ev Moses Kaplan?" Why was it whenever someone said my full name it was a threat? "All of the forces arrayed against you. Every ghoul, every warlock, every demon under the moon and sun tasked with tasting your blood. They call you a wolf; how ironic the name now, eh?" He laughed again, his face warping, stretching. Skin ripped open as hair the color of old blood and fresh rust broke through the meat as he transformed. His arms lengthened. I heard bones popping as he grew, and the rip of skin was sickening as claws tore from his fingers. He was larger, more terrifying than almost any creature I had seen before. Almost. I had met the eyes of far too many cosmic beings to break down into a puddle of fear at the sight of a mangy *drek lecher* like Peter Stübbe.

"You want to be like your namesake, Moses, and lead your people to freedom and safety, to have relationships, to bring about a new era ... but you won't. You die today. You think you came armed in piety, but you are no tzaddik, Ze'ev Moses, you are no saintly man." The last was growled through a maw like the nightmares children have. All long savage teeth and thick blood-flecked drool.

"No ..." I finally answered, dropping the canvas

bag and revealing a simple wooden baseball bat. "I am no Baal Shem Tov, I am Ze'ev Moshe Kaplan, and like my namesake, I will bury you in the fucking sand." I ran forward to meet him there in the street, swinging the bat as I went.

The bat wasn't just a baseball bat. It had been carved from the limb of an olive tree in Israel that had been severed by lightning. Over the course of years, I had inscribed in it the names of angels, anointed it with pure oils and prayers, engraving seals and psalms and prayers into the wood by the light of Shabbot candles. Across the surface, the name of the arch-angel Gabriel shone with its own light as I pumped my intention into the bat. My intention was never so clear.

He came at me, meeting me head on, but I had expected him to. I swung up as he swung down, and the bat connected with his right elbow in a resounding crack that echoed through the empty streets. Bone fragments burst from his arm. I could feel the rage of the angel of HaShem's strength blazing behind me. The thing that was Peter staggered back, clutching at his elbow. For the first time, I saw fear in his eyes. Fear of pain, fear of retribution, the fear brought by his arm not healing.

He was an old and stubborn thing, fast and deadly. His pain and fear were making him sloppy, while my rage and determination to rescue Sandy kept me razor focused on surviving. I ducked under his left arm as it swiped at me and then rolled back before his leg could connect in what I was sure would have been a life ending kick. He pressed what he thought was his advantage, coming at me with a savage back hand. I leaned back just out of reach and then stepped inside his swing. I swung the bat up as hard as I could, hitting him in the arm pit of his left arm. The shoulder broke messily, the bones grinding against one another as the entire shoulder blade fell unsupported inside his body. I'm sure a few of his ribs were destroyed as well.

He howled in pain and anguish, his arms hanging uselessly now — one broken at the shoulder, the other at the elbow. He could probably attack with his feet or try to rip my throat out with his teeth, but the fear he felt was clouding his mind from possibilities. He had gone from fight to flight. I didn't relent, I followed him as he retreated. He turned to run, realizing that he had underestimated the danger I represented, but I was already swinging and hit the knee of his back leg from the side. It broke. It broke in the most satisfying crunch of powdered bone and inhuman wail you can imagine. I swung again, catching the shin of his other leg as he fell. It broke too.

My arms burned. Much like with the sacred alefbet, my body was bucking against the use of the bat. It just wasn't designed to wield divine power. But I ignored the pain. Stübbe sprawled on the street, three limbs broken. It was a strange echo of his supposed execution on the wheel in the 1500s. He moaned horribly, blood leaking from the corner of his mouth.

He began to transform back into a human, well, a human shaped thing. He would beg for his life, he would beg to be spared. He wasn't a danger to me or anyone else now. But he was a child murdering monster who had hurt Rivkah. There were laws about preserving life ingrained deep into my psyche and into the Jewish people's collective memory. Do not kill, do not kill, do not kill. My hand squeezed the grip of my homemade bat. He couldn't hurt me now. I could take Sandy; we would be safe. For now, though, only for now. And what about the children he had already killed? What about Hailey? My vision was clouded from the adrenaline, from my anger. So many victims, so many Haileys and Kristens. And I had made a deal. Sandy's life for his. The deal didn't matter, not really. There was no other option. He may have looked human, but he was a monster.

I stepped past him as he began to blubber around the blood in his mouth, trying to form the words through the pain to convince me to spare him. I brought the bat down on his head with every last ounce of strength I had in me. When I pulled the bat back, pieces of what was left of Stübbe's skull, teeth, and bits of brain clung to the wood. He didn't heal, he didn't get up, and he would never laugh or hurt another child again.

I walked away from the corpse and put the bat back in its canvas bag. I would need to clean it, care for it soon. I took the time to pick up the casings from when I had been firing the gun. I wanted as little evidence as possible that I had ever been there. But now I just needed to get to Sandy, to free her and check on her.

Chapter 16

I nearly collapsed as I walked into the shade of the diner. My entire body ached, it hurt so bad. But I couldn't rest, I couldn't stop now. I gathered all the weapons and charms I had lost on my way to the back where Sandy sat, tears streaming down her dirty face.

When she saw me, her eyes grew huge, and I saw her shudder with the force of relief. I limped past her to grab my knife from where it had fallen in the battle. Once I had it, I easily cut through the leather straps that bound her to the chair. In seconds, she was up and gasping for breath. She turned, and I didn't know if she was going to scream at me or hit me. But instead, she hugged me tight, sobbing into my shirt. I reached up and rubbed her back. I understood the fear. I had been kidnapped by monsters before. It wasn't an easy experience.

"He killed her, he killed her and he took me." She sobbed.

I shook my head, giving her a squeeze.

"No, no, Rivkah's okay; she's at the hospital; she's alive."

"She's alive?" She didn't seem to believe me, as though she had resigned herself to the death of everyone. Knowing the werewolf's propensity for threats, he had probably spent time torturing her mentally.

"She's alive," I assured her. I considered that I left Rivkah with the Sheydim, but he had promised not to hurt her ...

"Is ..." She trailed off, swallowing a ball of fear, and sniffed loudly as she pulled away from me. "Is he out there?"

"He's dead."

"And the things? He was with these terrible—"

"They're gone too." I affirmed.

She leaned into me again, finally letting the full weight of her fear and relief come out in tears. After a few moments, I extracted myself from her.

"I have to take care of the body. I can't just leave it out there, it's ... it's going to be messy." I moved away from her and searched the kitchen until I found a large knife. I tested the edge; it would have to do.

I glanced over, and she was staring at me in near panicked fear.

"He's a werewolf. I don't know if he can come back from what I did, but I aim to make sure of it."

"Should I ... should I come with you?" she asked. "I'm supposed to learn this stuff?"

"No, you don't need to see what I'm going to do. You wait in here while I ..." I sighed. "While I do what I have to."

I left her there in the kitchen. I didn't actually know if anything could come back from what I had done with what I had done it with. But I did know that there were plenty of werewolf legends, legends that dealt with how to dispose of monsters to stop them from coming back. Stübbe had been executed and broken before, he had been beheaded before. I couldn't let him rise again, not this time.

I knelt on the asphalt next to his body and used

both hands to push the knife into his chest. It was disgusting work, work I would never want to get used to. But it had to be done. I tore through his chest and finally extracted his heart. I set it aside. Next, I started sawing at the neck. I had expected it to be worse, but there was so little left of his head that it didn't feel like I was cutting through a human neck. I set the remains of the head to the side. As quickly as my battered body allowed, I drug all the components of Peter Stübbe back behind the diner, to where the dumpster sat. A little searching around the side helped me find a shovel—probably used for compost or waste.

I dug until the sun was low in the sky. Three holes in three places, a large hole for the body and a small hole next to a small crossroads of footpaths for the heart. The last hole was a bit further, but I had dug this one the deepest. I found a fist sized stone and placed it in the ruined remnants of Stübbe's mouth before dropping the whole thing in the hole and burying it. By the time I was done, it was dark. The full moon above gave plenty of light as I went back inside to fetch Sandy. We had to reach Dell City proper; from there, we could grab a Greyhound back across Texas, back home.

✡

Sandy sat next to me on the Greyhound. We were getting a lot of stares from the few people that were on the bus, but there weren't too many. Just us, a couple of day laborers who traveled around looking for work, and an old man in black shades in the back seat of the bus noodling on an old acoustic guitar while smoking cigarettes. I was resting my eyes, trying to fall asleep on the long bus ride, but I could feel Sandy restless beside me. I didn't blame her. I had already called the hospital. Rivkah was okay. It had been rough, touch and go for a bit, but by the time I called, she was out of the woods. She had been more worried about Sandy.

"Is that even legal?" Sandy asked eventually as the smoker was starting a song about clay pigeons.

I cracked open an eye and watched the man playing for a moment. "He's a sheyd, they won't even notice him." I felt her stiffen in alarm. "Don't worry, he's a good one, just likes playing music and whiskey."

"Oh ..." She leaned her head against me. "Ze'ev? How do we tell the difference between the good guys and the bad guys?" she asked.

I let out a long breath, considering the question. "I wish there was a straight forward answer to that, Sandy, but we don't have it any easier than anyone else, you know? When you were in Memphis, how did you tell the good people from the people that might try to abduct a young woman?"

"I guess ... I guess I hoped for the best from everyone but was always careful, just in case. But with people, it's different, isn't it? Everyone is different, and there's no rules for what a person will be like."

"Well ..." I fidgeted in my seat. I didn't want to move too much. I was hoping she would fall asleep too, eventually. "The world of magic is exactly the same. Take Blaze back there. He plays his music on the backroads of Texas, rides the bus around, and occasionally stops when he rolls into a place with a bar. That's all. He isn't evil, not necessarily good, just ... he is who he is."

Blaze saw me looking at him and tipped his head towards me. As he did, I saw the slight glow of otherworldly light from behind the glasses. I returned the nod with a small smile before turning my eyes back to the window in front of me.

"We always have to be careful, but maybe, instead of trying to think of the magical world as being this mythic otherworldly thing, think of it as an extension of the natural world, supranatural instead of supernatural. Sure, there are animals and things that are dangerous, but most of it all just wants to exist."

"Sounds like ethics and philosophy," she said with a sigh.

"Non-Humanities," I teased. "There's another kid, maybe a little older than you, but he's in the same boat, thrust into the supernatural world and forced to be a part of something. It feels like it's going to drown you almost all the time. It feels overwhelming. But it's just a part of the world. I promise that those uninitiated also feel overwhelmed all the time. It helps to have a friend and people who can talk you through stuff." I made a mental note to invite Anthony to start joining us; community always helped.

"I don't know if I can handle all of ... all of this, Ze'ev."

"It isn't always like this. Usually it's just blessings and healings and the occasional dybbuk, and those tend to be more scared of everything than we are of anything. You'll get the hang of it."

"Promise?" she asked.

"Promise." I couldn't actually promise that. I knew that the future was always in flux, but I did know that I could help her not be blindsided by the scary shit. And I could help make sure the scary shit knew to back off. I was about to say something, but I felt her snore into my arm and decided not to interrupt her much needed rest.

I closed my eyes to follow her into slumber.

✡

I opened my eyes in Crisp, Texas. I was in the barn. Shadows swallowed everything, and I saw the red glint from the eyes of wolves in the deepest shadows, circling me hungrily. By the light that came in through the busted back door, I saw them.

Domah, my angelic instructor dressed in gold and white robes, he stood face to face with a terrible, desiccated man in a black suit. Other shapes resolved themselves in the murky light. The cyan and gold robes of Lillith, the shard of darkness that I had made the deal with, the olive skinned giant from the City East of Nod.

Lillith's eyes met mine, and my heart nearly burst from the love I felt for her, but in her eyes was only sorrow. The desiccated thing in the suit broke apart from the others and approached me. He smiled, standing there looking me up and down.

"You have done well enough, the best you could do. Not bad for dust, hmm?" His smile was painful to look at, the skin was so thin and stretched.

"Was there ever any doubt? The universe was made for me, after all," I said, too tired to be scared.

His eyes, milky and awful, widened at my retort. He laughed, and by G-d, I wish I had never heard the sound.

"Yes, yes it was." He shook his head and turned to glance back at the meeting of supernatural might he had left next to the doorway. His smile fell away. "Ze'ev, don't trust them. You'll forget everything else here, but try to remember this. Do. Not. Trust. Them."

✡

I woke up with a start, brought out of whatever dreams I might have been having by my phone buzzing with messages. We were passing through Austin city limits, which meant we were almost home. I would need to check on Rivkah in person and visit Alex, give him the news that the nightmare was over. Sandy was asleep in the seat next to me, curled into a little ball. I adjusted the small travel blanket the bus had provided over her and checked my phone. Two messages. One from

Sara, the other was from Mr. Grin. I frowned as I opened one and then the other.
They both had the same ominous message.

We need to talk.

John Baltisberger

About the Author

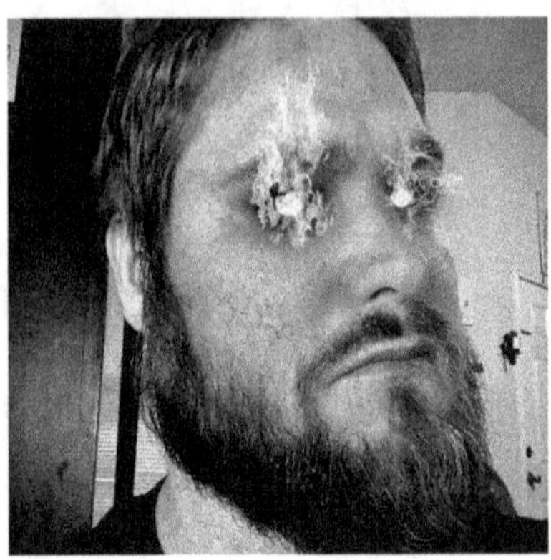

John Baltisberger is an author of speculative and genre fiction that often focuses on Jewish Elements. Through his writing, he has explored themes of mysticism, faith, sin, and personal responsibility. He lives in Austin, TX with his wife and his daughter.

Though mostly known for his bizarre blend of Jewish mysticism and splatter, John defies being labeled under any one genre. His work has spanned extreme horror, urban fantasy, science fiction, cosmic horror, epic verse, and he has even written a guide for mindful meditation. You can see his work and more at www.KaijuPoet.com

More Books from
Aggadah Try It

Treif Magic by John Baltisberger
isbn: 978-1-7348937-0-0

Of the Book: An Anthology of Jewish Horror
isbn: 978-1708473730

The Green Children Help Out by Gillian Polack
isbn: 978-1-955745-03-1

And Coming Soon!

Giant Robots of Babel
by Maxwell Bauman